THE
NIGHT ROOM

by E. M. GOLDMAN

PUFFIN BOOKS

PUFFIN BOOKS
Published by the Penguin Group
Penguin Books USA Inc., 375 Hudson Street, New York, New York 10014, U.S.A.
Penguin Books Ltd, 27 Wrights Lane, London W8 5TZ, England
Penguin Books Australia Ltd, Ringwood, Victoria, Australia
Penguin Books Canada Ltd, 10 Alcorn Avenue, Toronto, Ontario, Canada M4V 3B2
Penguin Books (N.Z.) Ltd, 182-190 Wairau Road, Auckland 10, New Zealand

Penguin Books Ltd, Registered Offices: Harmondsworth, Middlesex, England

First published in the United States of America by Viking,
a division of Penguin Books USA Inc., 1995
Published in Puffin Books, 1997

1 3 5 7 9 10 8 6 4 2

THE LIBRARY OF CONGRESS HAS CATALOGED THE VIKING EDITION AS FOLLOWS:
Goldman, E. M.
The night room / by E. M. Goldman. p. cm.
Summary: When a group of students uses an experimental computer program
that simulates their tenth high school reunion, they get an unsettling
look at their possible futures.
ISBN 0-670-85838-2
1. Virtual Reality—Fiction. 2. High Schools—Fiction. 3. School—Fiction.
4. Interpersonal relations—Fiction. I. Title.
PZ7.G56795Ni 1995
[Fic]—dc20 94-30727 CIP AC

Puffin Books ISBN 0-14-037253-9

Printed in the United States of America

It wasn't quite over. Not just yet. He had a score to settle.

He kicked the wastebasket next to his desk. With one wave, he knocked all of the books from his top shelf onto the floor.

Then he noticed the book that she had left behind on the floor. He picked it up and opened it. To my own sweet Sarah. *Her grandmother.* Forever, your Fred.

Michael smoked sometimes, although not often. His ashtray contained dice used for gaming. He removed them.

Carefully he ripped the dedication page into thin strips, making a nest in the ashtray. Touching a match to the strips, he watched her grandparents' names sizzle and hiss like infant snakes. He proceeded through the entire book that way.

At last, he tossed the covers into the wastebasket. It was done. Over.

Empty.

The blind computer monitor beckoned to him like a friend. He returned to his chair and answered its call.

He leaned back in his chair. Smoke from the love poems still filled his mouth and lungs, stung his eyes. He picked up an ordinary six-sided die and rolled it around in his hands.

No, it wasn't quite over. Not just yet. He had a score to settle.

He picked up a pamphlet that Sara had given him weeks earlier. It described Argus as creating something similar to a dream state.

There were dreams. And then there were nightmares.

He threw the die.

OTHER PUFFIN BOOKS YOU MAY ENJOY

TO THE CREWS OF THE
STARSHIPS ENTERPRISE

Ira was standing before the Banting High bulletin board.

"Good morning, Ichabod." The girl's voice was deceptively sweet. He caught a glimpse of wiry copper hair as a khaki-clad figure moved to stand at his right.

Tess. He didn't turn from reading the announcements. "Good morning, Mother Teresa." If Tess pushed him any further, he'd ask for her blessing.

With a muttered swear word, the girl moved on. Touché, he complimented himself. The warning buzzer hadn't even sounded, and already he'd drawn blood.

Actually, he didn't mind being called Ichabod. He'd come into the nickname when he hit his growth spurt. Ichabod Crane. Okay, he was tall and gawky, and he had a nose too big for his thin face. He had it on good authority (female) that some other female thought he was cute, only his authority refused to tell him which one.

Not Sandy Wilcox. Not a prayer.

THE NIGHT ROOM

"Just the boy I want to see." Ms. Ruddley was his Grade 11 Health teacher, and also a school counselor.

He froze into immediate guilt. "What did I do?" More likely, what hadn't he done? Whatever it was, he'd hand it in by the end of the week. Promise.

"It isn't anything you did," the slim black woman said. "It's what you're going to do. Stay here. Don't move. I have a treat for you in my office." She disappeared through the doorway.

First period started in fifteen minutes. A teacher had a treat for him. Sure. He glanced at the teachers' bulletin board, full of notices about meetings that looked like guaranteed snooze time. Someone had tacked up a stained gym sock with a note reading *Cinderella, where are you?*

Ms. Ruddley was back immediately with a sheaf of announcements. "Read the one on top. Or the one on the bottom. They're all alike."

Caught by the sight of his own name—galvanized by another that made his heart do wheelies—he began to skim the notice. He stopped and stared. "We're doing the Argus program now?" This was Star Wars stuff, the prototype of a computer program that was supposed to show them at their tenth high school reunion. Banting was one of the first high schools to try it.

"Just read the notice."

ANNOUNCEMENT

Date: November 28
Attn: Health 11 Class   *seven (7) students*

2

Re: Personal Development Unit

> Joy Abercrombie Ira Martinic
> Mac Collier Tess Norville
> Barbara Flores Sandra Wilcox
> Graham Hork

Your appointment with Argus is scheduled for 5:00 P.M. on Thursday, December 7. We will meet in the observatory parking lot at the university, and I will have a few words with you before we enter the waiting area. You will bring permission slips signed by a parent or guardian as well as completed medical forms.

Wear comfortable, loose clothing. Prepare for delays by bringing homework or other reading material of an uplifting nature. You will enter the Night Room one at a time. For maximum value, those who enter early are asked to refrain from discussing their insights with others waiting.

REMEMBER: Argus is a scientific program. Its purpose is to give you an idea of your possible future based on the individual interviews and questionnaires filled out earlier. Other factors are luck, aptitude, skill, opportunities, and the willingness to work toward a goal. The purpose of this program is to get you to ask questions, not to provide answers.

Life is a pie. You can choose the slice you want (although you won't necessarily get it). You can take whatever you're handed on a plate. Or you can let the dessert cart pass you by.

Edith Ruddley
Counselor   *cc: Dr. Ursula Halstrom*

THE NIGHT ROOM

VERY IMPORTANT: BRIEF MEETING
3:15 P.M. TODAY, RM. 101.

The lines about the meeting after school had been underlined in red.

"We're going through Argus next Thursday night?"

"Thursday," the teacher echoed. "I know this is short notice, but Dr. Halstrom's assistant just phoned me. The computer will be underutilized next week because of exams, so they're able to squeeze us in. Otherwise we won't have an appointment until spring. Do you have any problem with the time?"

He shook his head. His social calendar wasn't exactly full, and he was curious about this computer program that was supposed to foretell his future.

"I'll phone the university and ask them to give Barbara Flores a message about this afternoon's meeting," Ms. Ruddley said. "I believe you have classes with everyone else. Everyone except—"

"Sandy Wilcox." Ira always got a ringing in his ears from hearing her name. Speaking it made him breathless and giddy.

"Do you think that you can find her?"

"Sandra?" Ira wheezed. "Wilcox?"

"Sandra." The counselor paused. "Wilcox."

Bells chimed joyfully—carillons, not the strident buzzer that called students to first period homeroom. Ira heard little tinkling bells, huge dignified sumo-wrestler-sized bells. Bells jingled on the harnesses of Santa Claus's reindeer as they delivered gifts to deserving little boys. He also thought he heard "Twinkle, Twinkle, Little Star" played on a Fisher-Price xylophone, although he wasn't prepared to swear to that.

"Earth to Ira. Come in, Ira." Ms. Ruddley was looking at him peculiarly. "You'll find her standing near the entrance to the library. She's circulating a petition, I think."

He tried to take a shortcut up a down staircase, got stopped, and had to run down again through hordes of students. After the second staircase plus a three-quarter turn around the school, he suddenly saw her standing near the library door. Sandra Wilcox. His goddess.

Morning sunlight poured through the tall window at the end of the hallway, outlining her in flame, turning her fair hair incandescent. Blinding him, but that was okay because he didn't plan to use his eyes again. She was talking to two girls, probably about the petition she was holding.

Tess was also there, standing at a table near the library entrance, reading a Greenpeace pamphlet. In the bright sunlight, her hair shone like a new penny. "If you're trying to sneak up on me," she said when he came to a halt beside her, "I think you should know that you'd make a rotten spy. I spotted you on the stairs. So, what do you want now?"

"Nothing from you."

"Good. That's what you're going to get." She paused. "What do you really want?"

"Can't tell you. I've already sent my wish list to Santa. Anyway, it's X-rated."

"*You?*" She laughed. "PG-13, tops."

A lot she knew. He picked up an identical pamphlet. "I need to talk to Sandra. I guess she's busy."

"Sandra. I might have figured." She returned to her reading. "You are so obvious."

Am not. Are, too. He mentally filled in the blanks, then remembered something as they stood side by side, staring at their pamphlets. "I read your article about the science fiction convention you went to. It wasn't bad."

Tess worked on the school paper. Next year, everyone expected her to be editor. For a moment, she looked startled, then pleased. "It was good, wasn't it? Actually, that story was one of my favorites."

Her hair fascinated him. He wondered what it would be like to touch, whether it would be springy under his hands or soft. She looked almost pretty when she smiled, and that discovery puzzled him, too. Tess probably thought the flak jacket plus the camera hanging on a strap around her neck made her look like a real investigative reporter.

He had no idea why he was noticing these things when he was only a few feet away from the girl who occupied his fevered dreams. As Tess began to turn away, Ira remembered that her name was on the list. "Wait."

"What's this?" she asked as he handed her a notice.

"From Ms. Ruddley. I have to give one to Sandra."

"You do that." She began reading the announcement. "Go talk to Sandra."

He turned back toward the source of the light as a girl finished signing Sandra's petition. She moved away.

"Hi, Ira." Sandra smiled at him. Ira was afraid that he

would throw up, or worse. "I guess class is starting soon."

Her smile made him feel like he was standing in front of a warm fire. "Class," he croaked. "Soon." He glanced at the wall clock. Very soon. He held out an announcement. "I have something for you from Ms. Ruddley."

"Thanks. Have you signed our petition yet?" She held out the clipboard. "We plan to present it to the school trustees on Friday."

He'd sign ten times if she would smile at him again. One hundred times for a kiss. "Do you have a pen?"

She pointed at a pen attached by string to the clipboard.

Ira's ears grew hot. He had just made a fool of himself in front of Sandra. She had positive proof that he was an idiot.

He managed to balance the petition on top of his books as he signed, praying that everything wouldn't fall to the floor.

As he signed—what was he signing?

"How many signatures do you have so far?" Tess asked Sandra as she strolled up to them.

"Almost two hundred," the other girl answered. "There are still a few days left. Your story helped."

"Tell me if there's anything else I can do."

He scanned the top of the page rapidly. Day care. The petition asked for a classroom at Banting High to be used as a nursery so students with babies could return to classes.

"Too bad there aren't any extra classrooms," Tess said.

"It's a great idea," Ira said loudly. "Great."

Sandra's silver charm bracelet tinkled as she took the

clipboard from him. The charm bracelet had come from Patrick. Her boyfriend. They had been going together since the previous summer. Patrick was eighteen, a freshman at the university. Ira had seen them together, hand in hand, arm in arm, and on one horrible occasion, lip to lip.

He had to admit that they looked good together. If they were in a movie, Patrick would be cast as Sandra's surfer boyfriend. Just thinking about him gave Ira a headache.

Still, rumor had it that Sandra had a lot of free time on her hands lately. Ira was hoping that meant she and Patrick had broken up. He'd even been practicing in front of his mirror. *"I have a great shoulder to cry on, Sandy."*

Sandra's eyes sparkled when she looked up. "Next Thursday? That's great. I've really been looking forward to Argus."

"I'm coming that night, too," Ira said.

Tess gave him a sharp look, and he remembered that she was on the list as well. "I haven't decided whether I'm going," she said.

Sandra's next words stopped him before he could respond. "The timing is marvelous, too. I can't see Patrick because of Hell Week. He's really been hitting the books."

"Hell Week," he said flatly.

"Hell Week is what they call exam week at the university," Sandra explained. "Patrick has five finals."

The buzzer sounded. Tess turned to go. "See you later, Ira." Not Ichabod. But the red-haired girl's use of his correct name barely registered.

He sighed deeply. The only reason Sandra wasn't seeing her boyfriend was because he had to study.

It was after school, and five students had gathered in room 101. "There are still two girls coming," Ms. Ruddley said as they stowed winter jackets and books. "I'll give them a few more minutes."

"I gave Sandra the announcement," Ira said in case Ms. Ruddley thought he'd messed up. "I didn't forget her."

"I was sure you wouldn't." The teacher began sorting papers on her desk. "This has all been very last minute."

"You mean we're really going to do it?" Mac was grinning. "The simulation thing?" He was the biggest guy in the classroom, one of the biggest in the school. A football player.

"You're really going to do it," Ms. Ruddley said from the front of the room. "*You*, not me. I already know where I'm going to be when I turn twenty-eight. I'll be on a cruise heading somewhere hot."

That was a joke unless she planned to start aging backward. Ms. Ruddley had recently been given a surprise thirtieth birthday party by the other teachers at Banting.

"Before you ask," Ms. Ruddley said, "the other students in your class will probably be seen in February. I was told that your names were chosen solely because your interviewers had finished their paperwork. Still, this is quite an adventure. The program is new as far as high school students are concerned. You can consider yourselves pioneers."

"Guinea pigs," Tess muttered. "I don't know about this." She had taken a seat to Ira's right.

He was amazed she would even consider passing up this opportunity. It wasn't as though she was a coward. In the future, she would probably end up winning major awards for writing if she didn't get herself killed taking a close shot of an exploding bomb.

She had taken out her spiral notebook and was scribbling hurried notes in what looked like Egyptian hieroglyphs. Her coppery hair fell over her eyes. As she shoved it back, she scowled at him. "What are you looking at?"

"Not at you," he said gamely. "That's for sure." Actually, he didn't mind looking at Tess even though she dressed as though she was reporting from a war zone. He suspected that somewhere under all that khaki, she had a body that wasn't half bad.

He suddenly realized that Tess was looking him over from the top of his head down to his feet. Her gaze started back up again. He felt his face redden. "What?"

"I can't say that the view from here is all that great, either," she said at last.

"So either stop looking at it or take pictures."

"And break my camera?"

He was about to say something back. Then the door opened, and Sandra walked in. His mind immediately went into overload.

"I'm late," Sandra apologized. "I know I am."

"You're just on time. Take any seat." Ms. Ruddley looked around. "It looks like Barbara has been delayed, so we'll begin."

Sandra set her books on the desk in front of Ira's. "Ms. Ruddley, what do they mean exactly when they say they want us to wear comfortable clothes?" *Comfortable clothes* made Ira think of her wearing something thin and diaphanous, assuming that diaphanous meant see-through.

"Loose sweat suits are ideal," Ms. Ruddley answered, spoiling his dream of Sandra drifting toward him in something white and flowing. "Come in your jam-jams if you want to, as long as they're decent. Other questions?" She waited. "Don't be afraid to sound silly. We're all here to learn." She waited again.

Some classes at Banting were divided according to ability. Health wasn't one of those. That didn't keep anybody from knowing who the bright students were—also the other kind. The class I.Q. range started at Barbara Flores, a certified genius. It ended at Graham Hork.

As for Ira, he truly believed he belonged somewhere in that great bulge in the middle. Unfortunately, sometime in his early school career, a mischievous computer had messed up. He had been assigned intelligence test scores indicating that if he wasn't destined to find a cure for cancer or blast off to the stars, he should at least be able to coast through school.

Ha!

He got mostly Cs, some Bs, the occasional A. His report cards were filled with nagging computerized comments like *Try harder* and *If you use your class time wisely, you could complete your projects.* He wondered whether anyone was ever congratulated for living up to his potential. *Okay, Jimmy, you can go home early today. You've hit your potential.*

Maybe he'd give them all heart attacks someday and surpass his potential. Maybe that's what Argus would show him. Success, whatever that meant.

"Hey." Graham had been rereading his announcement at his desk. "Hey. Hey, Ms. Ruddley? I don't get it."

"Which part don't you understand?"

"All the words with more than five letters," Mac quipped.

Tess straightened and turned around. "Mac, I haven't seen your name on the honor roll lately."

"You haven't seen my name on the honor roll ever. And you're not going to." Mac sounded proud. "You're going to see my name in the Pro Football Hall of Fame." He turned toward the teacher. "This Argus thing will show that, right?"

Rumor had it that during football season, a scout had been looking Mac over from the stands.

"I'll take Graham's question first." The teacher nodded encouragingly.

The slight boy gulped. "I thought we were going to a party. Like, in the future."

Mac groaned.

Graham looked around at the burly football player. "Hey, I want to know, okay?"

"I want to know more about that, too." Ira thought he understood what was going to happen. Maybe not. Often his thoughts drifted when details were being explained. Tess glanced at him approvingly, although he had no idea why.

"You are going to a party," Ms. Ruddley said. "That much is true. But—" She hesitated at the sound of rapid footsteps in the hallway. "Can it be?" she asked as she headed toward the doorway. "Zounds, it is!"

Barbara Flores almost collided with the teacher, who dodged aside at the last second, thus averting a serious disaster—to Barbara. *Pixyish* was the term most often used to describe Barbara. She'd rounded out since she and Ira were sandbox buddies in kindergarten. Other than that, though, good old Barb hadn't changed much. She still looked as though she should be perched on a mushroom, wearing pointed shoes and a tassled cap.

"Sorry I'm late," the breathless girl said. "We were discussing solecisms and I forgot." She took the announcement from the teacher's hand and read it in two seconds flat. "This is it? That's wonderful."

"Sit," Ms. Ruddley directed. "We were just talking about what everyone should wear."

"Something really comfortable," Barbara said. "I've seen students waiting when I visit my dad in the Science building, and it's hilarious. One guy wore baby blue sleepers with feet. He even brought a teddy bear. Dr. Halstrom has no sense of humor at all. She refused to let him in until he apologized to Argus."

Apologize? To the computer? Ira could read the writing on the wall. This educational project was not going to be fun. It was going to be . . . educational.

"Barbara," the teacher said firmly, "sit down and get your breath. Let me explain to the others. Please feel free not to interrupt until I'm finished."

"Not to—?" Barbara stood there. "I understand." She sat and folded her hands. "What if you get something wrong?"

"Try not to snicker."

"Okay," Barbara said. "Go on."

Ira had decided long ago that Barbara was okay. She made straight As without studying. He suspected she couldn't help herself. Her mother was head of the university Mathematics department and her father ran the cyclotron. Barbara was widely rumored to be the by-product of a nuclear meltdown.

They were close friends going back to when he thought a genius was something that came out when you rubbed a magic lamp. Barbara was also the girl who had told him that some other girl thought he was cute.

The teacher began again. "In the Argus program, you will all attend a party marking your tenth class reunion. That means you will go forward eleven years. This is only a simulation. I'm sure you've all seen the holodeck in the *Star Trek* series."

Everyone nodded.

"The Argus program isn't anywhere near as advanced

as the holodeck On the other hand, it's here today, so you don't have to hang around until the twenty-sixth century."

"Twenty-fourth century." Barbara looked sheepish. "You were two hundred years off. That's a long time."

Ms. Ruddley seemed to be praying for strength from a god located inside the ceiling tiles. "You recall those interviews that you went through last month with graduate students."

There was a soft groan, instantly cut off. Barbara hadn't been at all impressed by her interviewer, the Twinkie.

"Argus produces highly realistic imagery constructed from input drawn from your interviews and questionnaires. You will each go into a darkened room when your name is called. In that room, you will find a reclining chair. It's quite comfortable, or so I'm told."

"Hey, Sandy," Mac said. "Would you mind coming with me when it's my turn? I'm scared."

"I don't think so," she answered quietly.

"If Mac or anyone else feels nervous about this procedure," Ms. Ruddley said, "there is no disgrace in dropping out."

Mac made a face. "A joke. I was joking."

"No joke. Many people don't care for the sound of the procedure. An apparatus will be put on your head. This is Argus."

"But it doesn't hurt." Joy Abercrombie sat on Ira's right. He didn't know her very well, although he'd seen her in the fall school play. She was plump, but not any more than he was skinny. Her statement came out as a question.

"No, it doesn't hurt." The teacher went on, "Up to this time, Argus has been used to assist college students with career and lifestyle choices. The program's creator believes that Argus will help younger students as well. As we grow older, we do not appreciate changes in ourselves because they come slowly. This broad jump into the future gives us perspective on our own behavior. Or so the literature says. We can see if we will become duplicates of our parents."

"No way." Graham looked pale. "There is no way that I'm turning into my old man." Graham's father, an abusive alcoholic, was in jail for killing another man during a brawl.

"I don't think you will," Ms. Ruddley agreed softly.

"I won't be anybody's punching bag, either." He leaned back, his color returning. "I'm going to do okay. I just want to see, like, should I take carpentry or maybe diesel mechanics. Or maybe something else." He looked worried. "If they've only been using the computer for college students, it's not going to try to make me go to college, is it?"

"College isn't for everyone," Ms. Ruddley said. "I've spoken with Dr. Halstrom, and she understands that."

"So we're going to be asleep," Mac said.

"A sort of sleep. Approximately twenty minutes of real time will pass for you here while you spend two hours at the reunion party."

Joy's hand went up again. "Will there be food? I mean, if you eat the food at the party, will you get fat? I'm trying to lose weight." She flushed.

Mac sniggered. "What about booze?"

"We'll be adults," Ira said impatiently. The reality of the

situation was becoming clearer to him. In eleven years they would be adults. Forever.

"I don't even want to think about how old I'll be," the teacher said. "The party will be held in a hotel ballroom. There will be food, and no doubt liquor. Since nothing actually exists, I believe it is fair to say that caloric consequences will be zilch. Remember, you are there to observe and learn. Don't use an expensive computer program to give yourself a hangover-free binge."

"Not me." Graham shook his head. "Nohow, no way."

"Another thing." Ms. Ruddley picked up the papers from her desk. "You will meet each other in the simulated future. That is, you will be meeting simulations of each other, only older. As far as everyone else at the party is concerned, eleven years have passed. If, say, Ira asks Tess for help on his History homework, she won't know what he's talking about. Okay?"

Tess turned toward Ira. "If you ask me for help here and now," she said, "you won't get it."

"Aw, Tess," Ira whined, "puh-lease." As far as History went, the teacher was interesting and they both did okay. They smiled at each other, then stopped abruptly.

"I can see that the natives are getting restless." Ms. Ruddley raised her voice. "I have forms here. The school district requires permission from your parents for you to go through Argus. The forms they signed earlier covered only the preliminary interviews. You will also need to see a doctor in the next few days so we can be sure you're healthy. There are instructions for you to follow next Thursday. You are to eat very lightly that day, nothing after noon except clear, nonalcoholic beverages. You can read the rest for yourselves. Last, but not least, there is a release required by the university."

"Release?" Mac said blankly.

"So you can't sue them if something goes wrong," Barbara piped up. "Sorry, Ms. Ruddley."

"What can go wrong?" Tess had that familiar look of a hound on the scent.

"Supposedly nothing," Ms. Ruddley said. "This is a requirement of the university." She looked around. Barbara had her hand up. "All right. Speak."

Barbara turned to face the others. "Usually the images are pretty much what you'd expect. But sometimes people see themselves living lives that aren't so great. You could end up feeling like you're in a bad dream—a very real one."

"What if I dream about a snake biting me?" Graham asked. "Would I be poisoned?"

"Nah," Mac said. "The snake would."

"You might feel sick for a while." Barbara seemed serious. "It's conceivable that a person with a heart condition could experience something so shocking that he'd die. That's why they have the screening process, to keep out people who are ill or unbalanced. Anyway, Graham, I don't think you have to worry about seeing any snakes at the party. Except Mac, of course."

"Let me say this one last time," Ms. Ruddley said. "While the concept of this program fascinates me, I am uneasy about students your age going through Argus. This has nothing to do with the program, but with your lack of maturity. In three years, you will be three years older."

Mac and Ira applauded. The others laughed.

Even Ms. Ruddley joined in. "Three years more mature, I mean. My feeling is that you'll benefit most from this program if you regard it as a fortune cookie. What's inside ain't necessarily so." She frowned. "Barbara?"

"This is sort of an open secret," Barbara said, "but Dr. Halstrom is working on Argus II. It's for people who have gone through the original Argus program. In this one, you'll be able to develop your own scenarios. It's a long way off, though. At least, I think so."

This was beginning to sound more and more like the holodeck.

Ms. Ruddley picked up her briefcase. "That's it, people. Go home."

Sandy looked at her watch. "Patrick is waiting for me."

"Hey, Sandra," Mac called as she headed toward the door with her books. "We have a date in the future "

She just laughed and hurried out.

"Eleven years," Mac said sagely, "can make a whole lot of difference."

"In your dreams," Ira said.

3

Sandra had decided not to say anything about the computer-generated program until dinner was over and her younger sisters had settled into their rooms. She brought up the subject casually while she and her mother were folding laundry together in the dining room. Her unsigned permission forms lay on the table.

"I'm not really comfortable with the Argus program," Mrs. Wilcox said as she finished a stack of towels. "Three hundred years ago, its creator would have been hanged for witchcraft."

"Argus doesn't claim to read the future," Sandra said.

"No? What would you call it?"

"A projection?" She hadn't meant her words to come out as a question. "Something that's possible."

"Possible or probable?" Her mother pulled a sheet from the basket and handed two corners to Sandra. They stood far apart.

"Ms. Ruddley says the choices are still up to us. And that other factors play a part. Luck. The economy. Technology."

"At your age . . ." Mrs. Wilcox fell silent as they folded the long sheet lengthwise. "I used to fold sheets like this with my mother. I always felt it was like a dance."

Sandra supposed it was a woman's dance, slow and stately.

Her mother ended up with the neatly folded sheet. "When I was a girl, it was my mother who held the sheets at the last." She was looking at Sandra in a way that seemed almost sad. "Someday, if God is willing, you will fold sheets with your own daughters. And sons." She laid the folded sheet on a chair, then brought another from the laundry basket. "But not for a while yet." She paused. "Did you mention Patrick to the university interviewer?"

Sandra stiffened. "A little," she admitted. "The questions were about my attitudes toward love and marriage generally. I think I said that I had a boyfriend."

"I'm not sure that high school students are mature enough for this program," her mother continued. "Suppose Argus shows you married to Patrick?"

She'd be seventeen in March. Her parents had become engaged when her mother was seventeen. "I suppose that's possible."

"I like Patrick," her mother said. "He's a nice boy. The problem is that people in love are so superstitious." Her mother stacked the newly folded sheets. "I can see how couples might marry because it's been preordained by a computer."

"Argus isn't superstition. It's science." Sandra had told the interviewer that although she planned to go to college, she hoped to marry early. She hoped to marry Patrick.

"Your father and I have already agreed that you can participate in this program." Her mother started toward the linen closet. "We just want to be sure that you keep some perspective, no matter what you see." She stopped. "What if Argus doesn't show Patrick in your future? Do you honestly believe that you won't feel differently the next time you see him?"

Patrick would be there.

He had to be.

4

"This is going to be so dumb," Barbara said to her mother. After the meeting she had returned to the university Science building, to the office her parents shared.

"Probably." Dr. Flores was expressionless as she regarded her daughter over a stack of student assignments. She had been unimpressed with Barbara's account of her preliminary interview.

Barbara chewed on her pencil eraser. "It will probably be interesting, too."

"No doubt," her father said. He was also Dr. Flores. Her parents were older than most, both over forty when she was born. As a result, they frequently treated her like a colleague. She was expected to make up her own mind.

The "reunion" would be a waste of time, definitely. She already knew what she planned to be. Much of her future was already mapped out. She didn't mind being surprised by the rest.

Still . . . dumb and interesting wasn't a bad combination.

"Who wants to sign my forms?" she asked.

Both Drs. Flores reached for pens.

* * *
* *
*

5

"I bought the groceries you wanted." Graham had come home from the market to find his mother asleep on the couch.

She turned so her face was toward him. "Put 'em away, will you, honey?"

"Sure."

"I'll get up pretty soon. I was just resting my eyes."

He went into the kitchen. Nothing had changed since that morning, including last night's dishes. Some days it seemed like she barely moved.

He'd bought some bread and eggs. A can of spaghetti. Milk was too expensive, but she said he probably wouldn't grow much more anyway. He'd be a small one like his dad.

His father had treated them both bad, real bad, but she still missed him.

She was sitting up slowly as he went back into the room. "How are your eyes?" Graham asked.

"Getting older. Like the rest of me." She yawned. "Shouldn't you be in school? What time is it?"

He told her.

"Lord, I must have been more tired than I thought. I don't see how I can watch so much TV when there's nothing on."

He tried to make a joke. "You can trade places with me and go to school."

She didn't laugh. "You can leave school anytime you want and get a job."

"Speaking of school . . ." Graham spoke casually. "There's this special program and I get to take part in it."

"What kind of special program?" She frowned. "You're not in any trouble, are you?"

"No!" He was shocked. "It's an honor. Sort of. Hey, there are only seven from the school taking part. One of 'em is on the football team, and one girl is running for student council. One of them is a girl whose parents teach at the university—she takes courses there and everything. There's a girl from the school paper." He couldn't think of the others.

"What do they want you for?"

"It has to do with this Health class we're all taking." His heart was thudding. If he tried to explain Argus to her, she'd never understand. He was having trouble understanding it himself, except that he wanted to see his future.

He had to know whether his future was worth sticking

around for. He couldn't end up like any of them. Not like his mom. Sure to God, not like his dad.

"There's these papers they want you to sign."

She leaned back again and shut her eyes. "That school sure does hand out enough forms. If it's not one thing, it's another." Her eyes opened. "How much is this honor going to cost me?"

"Nothing. It's free. They just want some high school students to take part." He went up and shoved the papers at her.

She let them fall into her lap. "If they want high school students so bad, they should be paying you."

"It's educational," he repeated. "I want to do it. It's only for one night."

"Wait," she said. "There's something here about a doctor appointment."

"A doctor at the university hospital will check me out. It won't cost anything."

He waited for her to ask why he needed to be examined at all. That was something he didn't understand too well. It was a requirement. That's all he knew.

She didn't even bother to pick up her glasses to read the forms. "If you want me to sign these papers, you'd better find a pen." He brought a pen from his knapsack and she scribbled at the bottom of the first page, on the line for the date, but he didn't suppose that mattered. She stood after signing the second one correctly. "If I have a son getting honors, maybe I'd better fix him some dinner." She looked around. "Did you pick up those groceries I asked for?"

He was used to her not remembering what he said from

one minute to the next. "I got 'em, Mom. They're in the kitchen."

She got on her feet slowly. "You're a good boy. I don't know why, but that's what you are." She started toward the kitchen. "Maybe you're too good for this world."

* * *
*
*
6
*

It was after dinner, and Joy lay on her bed reading the clippings in her scrapbook. She heard her mother's footsteps on the stairs.

"Joy? Are you up there?"

"Yes, Mama." Quickly she shoved the incriminating evidence under her bed so it was hidden by the flounced spread. "I'm"—she grabbed up a paperback book from her pillow—"I'm reading."

Mrs. Abercrombie approached the bed, then lifted the paperback to look at the title. "Oh, honey, not another diet."

Joy had spotted the book in the window of a bookstore the week before. "I thought I'd take a look at it."

Like her daughter, Mrs. Abercrombie was overweight. *Heavyset* was the term she preferred. She sat down on the bed. Joy could practically recite her mother's next words.

"Big bones run in the family." And her next words after that. "The doctor says you're perfectly healthy." The doctor had also agreed that she might feel happier if she lost some weight. "Twenty pounds over the norm is nothing to be concerned about. Besides, what is this world-famous norm? It's a number between some poor little anorexic and the circus fat lady."

"It's my body," Joy protested.

"I was miserable at your age, too, and for the same reason. For no reason. I made a good marriage, to your father."

Her father had died two years before, in a car accident. Last year they'd moved to Longacre so Mrs. Abercrombie could live near her family. In a short time, Joy had lost her father, her community, and all her friends. She knew she sometimes ate more than she should. All the popular girls at school had wonderful figures. She figured that she'd try to fit in with the local crowd after she managed to fit into a size 10.

"If you're trying a fad diet so boys will notice you, don't bother. There are men who like something to hang on to, not just skin and bones." Her mother paused. "The evidence of that is that I have a lovely family."

Joy and her brother both had *big bones*. Her slim younger sister Sally could eat anything without gaining weight.

"Mom, do you think we can drop the subject now?" Anyway, the problem wasn't just boys. It was everybody. Nobody wanted a newcomer who wasn't perfect.

Mrs. Abercrombie was on a roll. "Honey, you have beautiful skin and a very nice personality."

Joy winced.

"Don't make that face at me," her mother ordered sharply. "It just might freeze in that position. Then where will you be?" Her voice softened. "You did say that the boys danced with you at the cast party after your high school play."

They had. She had been almost too startled by the attention to enjoy it. She'd had a small part, a comic character role in a serious play. On opening night, the audience response was tepid for everyone else, but she received more applause than the stars "*Mom.*"

That was early November. Things were back to normal, meaning that she had returned to being invisible. To attempting to fill the gap with ice cream. Sometimes she felt as though she'd never be full again.

"All right, all right," her mother said. "Let me tell you why I came up here. While I was at your aunt Riva's, she mentioned that the church youth group is going caroling. They're raising money for repairs to the old church bus. You have such a nice voice—and you did go to that one meeting. . . ."

A meeting of people who had all known each other forever.

"You said they seemed nice." She began to speak more quickly. "I know you said you won't join anything until you lose at least ten pounds, but, well, this wouldn't exactly be joining. You'd be helping out. Besides, everybody will be bundled up against the cold. It should be fun."

Joy's voice wasn't so much good as it was loud. But she could carry a tune. Besides, with other people marching around in the dark, she wouldn't have to worry about what to say, how to make an impression

"Well?" Mrs. Abercrombie said

With a start, Joy realized that she was actually considering going. "I don't know. . . .'

"They'll be having a practice session on Saturday. Riva said that you know the songs, so she was sure you could join anytime." Her mother picked up the Argus pamphlet from the night table. "When you play this computer game next Thursday, how about giving me a phone call from the future?"

Joy smiled despite herself. "It's only a simulation."

"Even in a simulation, I will still be your mother." Mrs. Abercrombie began to rise, then frowned. She leaned down and pulled the scrapbook from under the bed. "Uh-huh." She laid the scrapbook on the bedspread. "You didn't tell these computer people that you wanted to be an actress?"

Joy's cheeks heated up. "We were supposed to mention anything we thought of."

"You want something steady. A hairdresser or a secretary." Mrs. Abercrombie was taking a secretarial course at the community college.

"The interviewer asked what I might want to be and what I would hate worse than death." Maybe she'd enjoy being a hairdresser. She would love to be an actress.

"It's fine to do what you want, but you have to think that a time might come—people might depend on you to clothe and feed them." Her mother stood again and headed toward the door. "In case you're interested, I'm baking cup-cakes. They'll be ready for tasting in an hour."

Joy groaned.

*   *   *

*   *

7   *

Tess's father was staring at his computer monitor when she slipped the permission forms in front of him. He had been in his home office since she got home at five. There was no sign of dinner preparations. At six he had come out and told her to find something in the freezer for dinner be-cause her mother was delayed at the office. He wasn't hun-gry.

Tess and her seven-year-old brother had eaten alone. Again.

"I need your signature for school," she told him.

He barely glanced at her. "You can sign my name."

"Okay." She took it away. "I can even talk to myself about why I don't like the project."

"What?"

"Nothing. I'll do it."

Mr. Norville's smile was distracted. "That's my girl."

She didn't leave. "What time is Mom coming home?"

"Hard to say," he answered after a minute.

"Do you want me to put Petey to bed?" She interpreted his nod as a yes. "Maybe I'll read to him. He likes *Charlie and the Chocolate Factory.*" No response. "You might try reading to him sometime. I bet he'd like that."

That earned her a glance. "I have a lot of work to do yet tonight. How about closing the door behind you when you go?"

She did. Tess went back in the living room, where Petey was sitting in front of the TV. "Well, I guess it's just you and me. How about hopping into your pajamas? We'll see what Charlie is up to."

8

"What's this for?" Ira's father asked as he examined the permission forms that night. They had just finished dessert, homemade apple pie—Mr. Martinic's specialty.

Ira paused from chugalugging a glass of milk. "It's for school. The Argus project."

"It's an experiment," his mother said. "Some doctor at the university is programming the kids and making them into robots."

"Hey, I'm in eleventh grade. I'm already a robot." Ira put down his glass. Stiff and mechanical, he walked into the stove. He clicked. Then he turned and headed toward his mother. Laughing, she dodged behind her chair.

Mr. Martinic took a pen from his shirt pocket. "Sounds good to me." He leaned the forms against the refrigerator and scrawled his signature. "Here," he said as he handed them back. "If you come back without a command installed about taking out the trash, I'm going to complain."

"Thanks, Dad," Ira said. He clicked again and jerked in what he hoped what was a robotlike manner.

His father clicked back. He struck himself in the forehead with his pen.

Mrs. Martinic reached into the cupboard and handed her husband a container of sewing-machine oil. "Enjoy," she said.

Parents.

"It's, like, a computer game at the university," Mac explained to his father before he left for school the next morning.

"Like an arcade game?"

"Educational." His dad seemed only mildly awake. He'd had a heavy night, judging from the lipstick on the cigarette butts in the ashtray. Mac had had a heavy night of his own with some of the guys. Right now his head felt like it should be left on the pavement and carted off by the city.

"Guess this program can't hurt," his father said at last. "At night, huh? What's the matter—they're not satisfied with sticking you in a desk for ten hours a day?"

"It's computer stuff," Mac mumbled. "Hey, your lady friend must've left early. I didn't see her."

His old man shrugged and headed toward the bathroom. "You didn't miss much. Some nights you take what you can get, right?"

Not yet, he didn't. It was time for Mac to leave for school, so he picked up his jacket. He paused outside the bathroom door. "Are you going to be around later?"

Water was running in the sink. "Hard to say. Why? Do you have something on for tonight?"

"Nah. I'll probably hang out."

"I don't suppose you've heard any more from that football scout."

"Not yet." Mac left for school.

* *
* *
* *

2

Michael Radford was working at the computer in his bedroom, had been for days, had slept three hours and then woke to curse three hours lost. Someone was knocking. Crap!

His mother, he assumed. Something about food. Laundry. Fresh air. Sunshine.

He was twenty, not mommy's little fair-haired boy. He was trying to concentrate, to force his thoughts back into rigid order like someone recovering from a fever. Interruptions only created more chaos.

The rapping became more insistent. "What now?" he

yelled without taking his eyes from the screen. The rent he paid should give him the right to work in peace. She couldn't even nag him about getting a job. When he was fourteen, he had developed a program that was a recognized part of virtual reality research. He had already earned all the money that he'd ever need.

The door opened slowly behind him. He tensed when he heard Sara's timid voice. "Your mom said it was okay for me to come up. She says you've hardly been downstairs for days."

He didn't turn, but he could see her shadowy reflection in the monitor. She was a slim girl of nineteen, her thinness accentuated by the blue work shirt she wore over her jeans.

"I've been busy."

"Your mother said—"

"I'm busy," he interrupted. Probably his mother had told Sara he wasn't eating. Probably she'd told her he hadn't slept since Sara broke up with him, either, except that his mother could only guess about that.

He hit the wrong key. Damn!

Abruptly he swiveled around in his chair to face her. Sara cringed back, her eyes wide in her pale face.

"So why are you here?" he demanded.

Sara moistened her lips nervously. "I'd like that book of poetry I loaned to you."

What book? Then he remembered the thin volume of love poetry that used to belong to her grandmother. He'd had it for maybe four months. Sara had planted it on him.

"Oh, Michael." It wasn't that he didn't read books. He read lots of books. Technical manuals, not poetry. *"Just take*

a look at them." Her smile had been sad. *"Honestly, it won't hurt at all."*

"Right." He tried to remember where it was, then spotted it in his shelves next to a well-thumbed volume on computer viruses.

He stood, holding the book close to him so she had to move nearer to take it from his hand. Neither he nor Sara was particularly tall, one of the first things he had noticed about her. The girls who were his height always seemed to be looking for basketball players. Sara treasured brains.

Right now she was as cautious as that alley cat that his mother used to try to tempt with hamburger. She seemed ready to dart away at any sudden motion. He forced himself to speak quietly. "Sara, you're being ridiculous."

She hugged the book to her chest. "No, I don't think so."

"You can't believe everything that Argus told you." His voice was getting louder. "You know that. Argus is about as scientific as . . . as the daily horoscope." Too late, he remembered that Sara read her forecast every morning. "You're too smart for that."

He wasn't a student at the university, but he came onto the campus often to use the library or hear the occasional lecture. He'd met Sara there the previous December. On the seventh.

He'd been interested when he first heard of Argus, which he judged to be in the early stages of development. After Sara said she was signing up, he looked into it more closely. The Finstater Foundation didn't use the university's mainframe, so he'd strolled in one day to take a closer look. He already had the access codes for every part of the campus, but in this case all he did was look like he belonged there, then wait until the program director went out for a smoke.

He'd figured that Sara would find the program interesting. It was supposed to identify trends that students might want either to concentrate on or to avoid.

For her, it turned out that he was somebody to avoid.

Because of a computer program, she had broken up with him.

He had no idea how to say she was gullible without showing how furious he was. Instead, he reached toward her, stopping when she backed away. "Come on. We'll go out for a bite to eat. I've been staring at the screen too long, anyway."

He hadn't. He was in the middle of something.

"Come on," he coaxed. He tried to put his hand on her arm but instead ended up with his fingertips brushing the book. "I'll read your poems, okay? Hey, maybe I'll even write a book report." His feeble joke went flat.

She stood firm. "I don't know nearly as much about computers as you do. And I know that Argus doesn't read the future. But it *saw* me. Michael, I could see myself." Her voice was becoming stronger. "I've always been attracted to boys with tempers. You fit the pattern."

He had already told her that he didn't fit anybody's pattern. Michael was superior. He'd spent his entire life being accelerated through school until he dropped out from sheer boredom.

"Michael, I've decided that I need counseling before I get involved with anyone else."

"I've never hurt you." He hadn't, but right now his fingers itched to grab her and shake sense into her.

She took a step back. As she knocked against the doorjamb, the book fell out of her hand onto the braided rug. He put his foot on it. "Stay," he pleaded, even though he was humbling himself. "Please, Sara. Or let's go somewhere and talk. We can work this out."

"You said you wouldn't go into counseling with me."

"I don't need counseling."

"Everybody needs help sometimes."

All he needed was her. No, not *needed*. He didn't need anything. He wanted her. Like he wanted air or water.

"Sara . . ."

She had knelt to pick up the book. He knelt with her, feeling as though they were in church with her book of love poems between them. The screen-saving function on his computer had darkened the blue screen. He could still feel it there behind him, looking over his shoulder.

He heard footsteps on the stairs.

"I didn't come alone," Sara said.

So that was it. She'd found another guy. Michael shot to his feet, and the book flew across the rug toward the door. He followed it, jerking the door wide so that it scraped across the book jacket.

Outside stood a second girl, a stranger. "Hi," she greeted him warily, "is Sara here?" As though she weren't a few feet away. "Sara, you said—we're going to a movie. . . ."

This was obviously something the two girls had set up between them. Sara stood shakily and nodded, then headed toward the hall. She turned. "Michael, please take care of yourself." She was still speaking as he slammed the door shut so he didn't have to look at her face anymore. Even so, he could still hear her last two words. "I'm sorry."

He stood there staring at the door. Damn her! He kicked the wastebasket next to his desk. Damn! With one wave, he knocked all of the books from his top shelf onto the floor.

Then he noticed the book that she had left behind on the floor. He picked it up and opened it. *To my own sweet Sarah.* Her grandmother. *Forever, your Fred.*

Michael smoked sometimes, although not often. His ashtray contained dice used for gaming. He removed them.

Carefully he ripped the dedication page into thin strips, making a nest in the ashtray. Touching a match to the strips, he watched her grandparents' names sizzle and hiss like infant snakes. He proceeded through the entire book that way.

At last, he tossed the covers into the wastebasket. It was done. Over.

Empty.

The blind computer monitor beckoned to him like a friend. He returned to his chair and answered its call. The monitor welcomed him with its brilliant blue light.

He leaned back in his chair. Smoke from the love poems still filled his mouth and lungs, stung his eyes. He picked up an ordinary six-sided die and rolled it around in his hands.

No, it wasn't quite over. Not just yet. He had a score to settle.

THE NIGHT ROOM

He picked up a pamphlet that Sara had given him weeks earlier. It described Argus as creating something similar to a dream state.

There were dreams. And then there were nightmares.

He threw the die.

Ms. Ruddley counted their cold red noses in the university parking lot. "All present. How is everybody feeling tonight?"

The sun had been down for almost an hour, and the temperature had fallen with it. Ira didn't know what the others had on under their coats, but the comfortable clothes he wore weren't exactly intended for winter conditions.

Sandra shivered. "It's c-cold."

"I'll warm you up, Sandy," Mac offered.

Ira had managed to inch over to stand next to Sandra. Startled when Mac spoke, the blonde girl bumped into him. He felt like her protector as he stood between her and Mac. "It's nice out here," Ira said. "Toasty."

"I won't keep you outside unless you insist." Ms. Ruddley frowned. "Tess, you do understand that no photographs may be taken inside. You'll have to leave your camera in the car."

Grumbling, Tess went back to lock her camera in the trunk.

"That's fine," the teacher said when she returned. "All right, boys and girls. We are about to go inside." No one applauded, possibly because all hands were shoved deeply into coat pockets or tucked under their arms.

"Again, I urge you all to be on your best behavior. While the procedure itself only takes twenty minutes, delays may occur for a number of reasons. One reason is that a level of relaxation must be achieved by each participant. That state could be chemically induced. However, the school district isn't about to agree to having its students stuporized."

Tess muttered something.

"What did you say?" Ms. Ruddley asked. "Tess, was that you?"

The red-haired girl raised her voice. "I still haven't decided whether I want to go through with this."

"Chicken," Mac said.

Ira clucked, then stopped right away. Mac picked up where he left off. He stopped, too, at Ms. Ruddley's scowl.

"If you two roosters want to stay here in the parking lot, you're welcome to do so," she said. "The rest of us are going inside where it's warm. I want to repeat right now that if anyone—at any time—wants to back out, he or she is urged to do so. This is not a contest of wills. All right?" She waited. "All right."

They were silent as they passed through double doors that led into brightly lit corridors smelling of recycled air. Directly inside, notices were tacked on a bulletin board about books for sale, students willing to tutor other students, an apartment to be shared. Sandra loosened her trench coat. She was wearing a turquoise sweat suit with pink and ivory trim, and a turquoise hair band.

Ms. Ruddley's voice had become quieter. "Except for a few evening classes, we're pretty much the only ones here. Nevertheless, you are asked to keep your voices down, particularly after the procedure starts."

Joy shivered. "That word," she said when the others turned to look at her. "*Procedure*. I don't like it."

There were dental procedures and surgical procedures. The word wasn't one of Ira's favorites, either.

Ms. Ruddley turned left when she reached a sign reading LAB 1, and the others followed like baby ducks. She led them into a large open room with straight-backed chairs along one wall. The room also had two wooden desks (one stacked with old magazines), a blackboard, and a huge cardboard box filled with toys next to a pile of exercise mats. In the corner stood a television and an ancient VCR on a shoulder-high stand.

"Welcome to the Argus project." A slender young woman in a lab coat came through a narrow hallway marked DO NOT ENTER. "I'm Karen Narita. You may call me Karen." Her long black hair was held by a clip at the nape of her neck. She spotted Barbara, and her smile became warmer and less formal. "I see that you and your friends made it here all right."

Graham was already looking around like he didn't understand.

"In case you're wondering about the furnishings, we share this area with prenatal classes and a well baby clinic and whoever else needs the premises. Argus is down the hall. You'll be entering the Night Room, a soundproof area the size of an ordinary school classroom—not surprising, since it used to be one. Argus will be monitored from an adjoining room by Dr. Halstrom. I'll be there as well."

"Will we get to meet Dr. Halstrom?" Tess asked.

"Probably not," Karen answered. "She seldom speaks with student participants."

"So you're, like, our hostess?" Mac asked her. "Will there be any food while we're waiting?" He looked around. Ms. Ruddley was rolling her eyes. Barbara seemed to be trying not to laugh.

Ira sneaked a look at Sandra. Her expression showed interest in what was happening, but her mind seemed elsewhere.

"I'm Dr. Halstrom's assistant," Karen stressed. "*Hostess* isn't included in my job description. Regarding food, we ask that you not eat until you're finished. You'll find a water fountain in the hall next to the washrooms, but you should restrict yourself to sips. Do not go in with a full bladder."

"She means that you might wet your diapers," Ms. Ruddley explained. "We went over that part earlier."

"I'll take your signed forms now," Karen said. "I also need to ask whether anyone has started a new medication in the last few days. Or whether you are using drugs, legal or otherwise."

Ms. Ruddley had already collected the forms. She handed them over.

"All right," Karen said. "In a minute I'll take you down the hall and show you the Night Room. Dr. Halstrom will be returning to the control area shortly. You won't be able to see her. However, she will hear and see you." She began to turn away. "You can hang up your coats now. I'll be right back."

Mrs. Ruddley waited until Karen was gone before she spoke. "I know you're all nervous, but cute comments must stop once you go down that hallway. The doctor has devoted her life to this project. She, and it, deserve your respect."

Barbara leaned closer to Ira. "Argus," she intoned softly, "is Dr. Halstrom's ba-a-a-by."

"I'm somebody's baby, too." At first he didn't realize that he'd spoken aloud; then he saw that the others were looking at him. No one laughed.

"Goodness," Ms. Ruddley said a few minutes later. "I feel so formal." Their instructor wore jeans and a brown turtleneck sweater. "The rest of you look like you're at a pajama party."

Everyone else had on sweats of some kind. Barbara's navy sweats identified her as part of the university Math department. Graham wore tattered loose jeans and a torn blue sweatshirt that looked as though he'd worn it while changing oil. Tess wore gray sweatpants and a baggy sweatshirt that were almost identical to Ira's, right down to the grass stains on the knees. BANTING HIGH was emblazoned across their respective chests. She wore a khaki shirt over hers, so that all Ira saw was ANTI HI.

Mac gawked at Joy. He threw his arm over his eyes. "Help me! I'm blind!"

Joy's sweats were bright orange. "I borrowed these from my mom," she said miserably. "She goes walking in the morning with some other women, and they like to be visible."

Joy was definitely visible. She could probably be seen from space, like the Great Wall of China.

"If you wore those at Halloween," Mac started, "you could end up with a face carved on your—"

Sandra was leafing through a women's magazine. She glanced up, frowning.

"Hey, look," Ira said loudly. "I see a bunch of tapes with the VCR."

"Educational, I'm afraid." Karen had returned. "You're welcome to watch them. And no, we're not on cable. Now, please follow me, and I'll show you the Night Room."

Tess went first. Ira and Mac brought up the rear.

"You may wonder why this is called the Night Room," Karen said as they stood looking slowly around the bare classroom.

"It's black," Graham said. "Everything is black."

"Well, duh." That was Mac.

Walls, curtains—even the windows—were painted black so no light could peep in. The room had the kind of half-light that Ira associated with sitting in a theater, waiting for the main feature to start. All illumination came from recessed ceiling fixtures. A meshwork design over the black overhead tiles looked almost decorative, although he knew better. The floor was shiny black linoleum, the blackboards black instead of the usual dark green. Near the walls were a few black metal cabinets, a high stool. In the dead center of the room was a dentist's chair.

Yikes! Nobody said it, but all at once they seemed to have their mouths firmly closed.

"Uh-huh." Ms. Ruddley pressed her lips together.

Okay, maybe not a dentist's chair, although he could see that it went back like a dentist's chair. It looked like it could also go up and down. He wasn't about to guess at the purpose of the attached electronics. In movies he'd seen hostages wired to bombs that looked more friendly.

He scanned the rest of the room in an effort to keep his teeth from chattering, then wished he hadn't. Discreetly tucked away in a corner was a wheeled cart with equipment that looked like it should belong to an official state torturer. The long electrical cord attaching it to the wall was as thick as a garden hose. *Aw, jeez.*

Karen intercepted his gaze. "That's emergency equipment. We've never needed it, but it's here just in case."

In case of what? No one dared ask.

"The university hospital is just down the road. I'm telling you that to reassure you."

Did he feel reassured? Ira wasn't sure.

"I'll show you our twinkle lights." She walked to the wall, to a light switch that was almost invisible. As the recessed ceiling fixtures dimmed, tiny lights came on at irregular intervals, shining with varying intensity.

"Like stars," Graham breathed.

"Many people consider this like the show at the planetarium." She put the lights up again. "Now for the scary part." She walked to the chair. "Some people thrash around or turn over in their sleep. Since you will be in a state very much like sleep, we have to use these."

Because everything was black, Ira hadn't realized that the chair had attachments. She unclasped a three-point harness going across the center. "This used to be a seat belt from a Lamborghini. That's a little humor to set you at ease."

"A seat belt," Mac said. "That sounds okay. So we won't fall on the floor, right?"

"We don't want you to hurt yourselves. People react differently to their experiences under Argus. There are padded straps for your wrists. Before I totally freak you out, let me emphasize that you can release yourselves at any time that you are wide awake. You are not truly confined."

Graham's words could barely be heard. "This is okay, right?"

"Nobody likes this part," Barbara reassured him.

"Hundreds of college students have been through Argus." Sandra spoke calmly. "Patrick took part last spring."

"It doesn't hurt," Karen said. "But you might scratch yourself. You could even break your own nose." She looked at them. "Most of us have no experience with confinement beyond being sent to our rooms as children. If you're truly bothered by this aspect, you may not be a candidate for Argus."

"Sounds kinda kinky," Mac said, but Ira thought he sounded nervous. "Will you stay with me, Karen?"

"I'm not sure that I could trust myself if we were left alone," the young woman answered pleasantly. Mac grinned. "No, I'm afraid not. Any other questions?"

"What about driving home afterward?" Sandra asked.

"Good question," Ms. Ruddley said. "Karen?"

"Students leaving Argus often feel slight confusion. If you're planning to drive, we advise you to return to the waiting area for half an hour. If you feel any doubts, don't drive."

"I'll be here until the last," Ms. Ruddley said. "If anyone needs a ride, I'm available as taxi service. I don't believe your cars will be impounded if left here overnight."

"They won't. Anything else?" Karen waited "Then we'll go back."

Ira didn't think he was the only one who felt relieved to leave the Night Room. The students didn't exactly sprint down the hall, but they jammed up at the door.

Karen came into the waiting room with them "It is vital for you to understand that Argus only shows possibilities. You are not seeing your future. The future has not yet happened. Everyone here still has full control over his or her destiny." She seemed to remember something "Applebanana."

They all looked at one another. "Sorry?" Ms. Ruddley said.

"Applebanana. Does anyone know what I'm referring to?"

"Fruit?" Sandra guessed.

"In a play," Joy said, "that's what you say when you want to look like you're talking. For crowd scenes."

"I know," Barbara said. "Some people have tried to use their turns to find out information about the future. Like, about the stock market or horse racing or who will win the

World Series in eleven years. If you ask specific questions, you'll get answers, all right. But all you'll hear is the name of a fruit or vegetable."

"Another thing," Karen said. "This is a reunion party. There are only seven of you. You will see people who look familiar, but you may not be able to put a name on them."

"Typical for reunions," Ms. Ruddley said. "I can personally vouch for that."

"We've already interviewed students from other classes who may be there in a minimal way. Some of you may have spouses in the future. Pay attention to the way you treat your partners and the way they treat you."

"Spouses?" Graham said.

"Argus attempts to identify trends in relationships, so you may be married." She looked at her watch. "Dr. Halstrom should be ready, so we might as well begin. Joy Abercrombie?"

"Here." Joy raised her hand slowly.

"Are we in, like, alphabetical order?" Mac asked.

"Not very original," Karen admitted. "But yes."

"So I'm, like, second?"

She nodded.

"I'm not in any hurry," Joy said nervously. "My homework is caught up and everything. Somebody else can go first."

"You don't have to go at all," Tess told her.

"I'm a little nervous," the plump girl admitted.

"We're more used to you being a bundle of joy," Mac said. "A bundle of Joy, get it?"

Ira supposed he wouldn't mind getting the whole thing

over with except that he would lose this excuse to hang around with Sandra, who was last. She had taken a chair and was leafing through her magazine. "It's interesting, huh?" he said.

"Mm."

He wished that she'd talk more. Maybe he and Tess tended to snipe at each other, but they never seemed to run out of words.

Karen cleared her throat. "Argus is programmed to deal with groups. Students have their turns in a specific order, always alphabetical. While anyone may withdraw at any time, it is not possible for the order to be changed."

Joy sat there, motionless and pale.

"You were really good in the school play," Barbara told her. "Argus doesn't bother me, but I don't think I'd have the nerve to go out on the stage in front of all those people."

Joy put back her shoulders as she stood. "I'm okay. I'm fine." They watched her as she headed down the hall. The image that Ira held in his mind was that of a caged canary being taken down into a mine. If the songbird didn't die from poison gas, the miners knew they would be safe.

"Better her than me," Mac said.

* *
*
*
*
2
*

"Are you comfortable?" Karen asked as the lights began to dim inside the Night Room.

"I'm okay." Joy barely whispered the words. The chair was fine once she got used to the idea of the restraining straps. At least they weren't really tight. Karen had already told her that she could lean forward if she ever wanted to.

"Now concentrate on the tiny lights that are coming on. They're very pretty, aren't they?"

"Mm-hm." She moved her toes, just to be sure that she still could. She had been instructed to leave her shoes in the hallway, and that hadn't been mentioned beforehand. Karen had given her cloth booties to keep her feet warm.

She wished she hadn't worn her mother's sweat suit. She must look like a beached orange whale.

The assistant went behind the chair where she could no longer be seen. Joy tried to turn so she could watch her.

"Stay still, please." A drawer slid open, then closed.

"I'm bringing out Argus now," Karen said in a hushed voice.

She came out with something held carefully in her two hands as though it were made of delicate crystal.

"That's it?" Joy felt strangely disappointed.

Karen smiled. "It looks something like a bicycle helmet, doesn't it?"

It looked a whole lot like a blue bicycle helmet except for the wire extending from the top, plus some kind of black knob.

"Of course, a real bicycle helmet would also cover the back of your skull."

"What about my hair?" She could feel her pulse hammering in her throat as Karen slipped the unit over her head and began to fasten the strap under her chin.

"You'll probably want to comb it afterward."

What Joy meant to ask was whether her hair would get in the way with the connection Argus made with her brain. She didn't want to ask for fear of seeming stupid, but she had thought that they might want to shave parts of her scalp.

"You can sit back now. Good. I'm going to make the chair tilt backward. Most people tense up when I ask them to relax, so I won't." Joy closed her eyes tight, then opened them again when the movement stopped.

Karen adjusted the strap under her chin, rechecked her wrist coverings. She sat on the stool and picked up a clipboard. "Try not to nod off. You'd be surprised how many people do."

Nod off? It was all Joy could do to release her death grip on the armrests.

In Drama, the teacher had taught them some simple relaxation techniques. As the room reached the level of dusk, Joy's breathing became steady and even. She yawned.

"Getting sleepy?"

"Um."

"You're probably going to be a really good subject."

"Have you done it?" Joy asked. "Gone through Argus?"

"No."

"Why not?"

"I don't want to." The answer seemed brusque, and Joy wondered if she had said something to annoy the assistant. Karen's friendly tone returned. "I'm going out now so my presence won't disturb you. Okay?"

"Hm." The chair was really very comfortable. The sky— no, the room—had turned an inky blue. Overhead, fireflies darted and danced. "Karen?"

"What?" The assistant stood near the door.

"Karen?" What had she wanted to ask? Oh, yes. "How will Argus know when I'm ready?"

The answer seemed to come from a long way off. "Argus will know." The door clicked shut, and then the room was still.

The lights. She watched the lights. As she lay there, Joy began to hear a faint humming, like bees taking nectar from her mother's prize roses.

The sound faded into the buzz of conversations, at first far away, then more distinct.

"That food looks almost good enough to eat," a man's voice said.

Joy had to blink in the unnatural brightness of the hotel ballroom. She was standing near a buffet table. Next to her, a gray-haired man in a suit was reaching toward a serving dish. He looked like a Banting Science teacher, but older. Unsure of what to do, Joy smiled nervously.

He smiled back. "It's nice to see so many of my former students again."

"You, too." As he moved away, Joy looked around. She was actually at a party in a hotel ballroom. Not *actually* actually, but it looked real. Chandeliers twinkled overhead. She heard music coming from somewhere, then realized that live musicians were playing a piano and string bass in one corner. A few people seemed to be looking at her.

Confused, she gazed down again at the long buffet table. It was filled with plates of scrumptious-looking food. Maybe she should eat something. She was positive that Karen must have heard her stomach screaming its demands.

Joy picked up an empty plate, then moistened her lips with her tongue. Her lips felt greasy, as though she'd been piling on Chapstick.

A woman moved to her left. "Oh, can I have your autograph?" she asked. "It would mean so much to my daughter."

Curious, Joy looked up. Directly opposite her stood a blonde beauty-queen type, with hair piled high. She wore an electric blue dress slit way down in front. Her chest was huge.

Obviously a classmate had become famous. It wasn't polite to stare, so she ignored the beauty queen and moved down to a stainless steel server holding chicken wings. She was reaching for the tongs when the same woman touched her arm. Joy started.

"I was positive that you hadn't heard me." The woman held out an autograph book. "If you could just sign here, Joy."

Across the table, the same woman was holding out a book to the blonde. Joy looked directly down into her own cleavage, barely covered by tight-fitting blue fabric. "Oh, my gosh!" She was as big as an aircraft carrier. She thought she recognized a mole at the top of her left breast, but nothing else looked familiar. She looked up again. The wall was mirrored. She was the beauty queen. This was what Argus saw for her.

She almost giggled. "What do you want me to write?"

" 'To Helen.' That's my little girl."

"Uh-huh." Joy wasn't sure what she scrawled, but the woman seemed satisfied. As soon as she left, Joy stood sideways before the mirrored wall. It wasn't just her chest. Her face . . . suddenly she couldn't recall what her own nose looked like. Everything was new and improved. Some areas ballooned out. Others were scrunched in so far that she could barely breathe.

"Joy." A young woman appeared at her side. "I was in your English class. That is, I was in the English class after yours for a while, but I sat in your desk. I saw your last two films—in fact, I saw *Vegetable Soup* five times." She thrust a reunion program toward her. "Could you give me your autograph?"

She had made it! She was an actress!

"Maybe you could write 'To Hilary, my former class-mate.'"

The only Hilary she knew was a girl who scowled at her if she tried to stay at her desk to write down the next day's assignment. Joy took the book. She looked for a surface on which to write, then bent over the table.

The tight dress slipped down even further. Around the room, men were gaping at her. Grown men. Some of them stood next to women who looked annoyed. She wrote her name, then handed back the book with a smile.

"Will you be bringing out another exercise tape soon?" the woman asked.

"Yes." She hoped it didn't sound like a question.

"Is it true what the tabloids say?"

"Which tabloids?" Joy sucked in her breath in ecstasy. Articles about her had been written for the supermarket tabloids. "What do they say?"

"About your diets?"

Oh. "Tabloids exaggerate," Joy said. That seemed safe. "Do they say anything about romance?"

"Well, I don't actually buy—" Hilary stopped. "All right, there was a copy of the *Enquirer* where I had my hair done. In fact, I tore out the article." She reached into her purse and began to read. "'Despite her knock-em-dead good looks, Joy considers herself a home type. She says she's shy.'" A man was gesturing at Hilary to come join the group of people he was standing with. "That's my husband. Thank you again."

Joy stood there. Surely she couldn't still be shy. She was

perfect. Talented. She had always assumed that once she took off weight, once people began recognizing her talent, everything else would fall into place.

She looked around in a daze, wondering who she could talk to about what was happening. In a way she had felt relieved that she would be the one to go through Argus first. That way she wouldn't have to make conversation with the others in the waiting area. Now she wanted to talk to the members of her class.

The first one she spotted was Graham, or a grown-up version of Graham. He stood near the bar talking to a thin woman who was probably their age, although she looked older. He wore a sports jacket that seemed ill-fitting and not entirely up-to-date. Like many of the others, he glanced in her direction and then looked away. Maybe he didn't recognize her.

Of course he didn't recognize her, she scolded herself. How could he when she hadn't recognized herself?

She thought she saw Tess's red hair. She was just moving in that direction when a man stopped next to her. "Hey, Joy," Mac's voice boomed. "I bet you don't remember my name."

"Mac," she said. "You're Mac."

"You remember." His face lit up. "How about that?"

She didn't want to see Mac. She hated having to be a good sport while he made coarse jokes. But he wasn't making crude jokes now. He wasn't moving away, either. "So, Mac," she said, "how have you been?"

"Can't complain. I see your name around often enough." He winked. "And your picture."

She wanted to be a serious actress. Surely she hadn't posed for *Playboy* or anything like that.

"You've really changed," Mac said. "Who would have figured?"

Not her. That was for sure. "Mac," she said, "we used to have a Health class together. Do you know what happened to the others? I spotted Barbara over there. What's she been doing?"

His answer surprised her, so she asked him about a few of the others. Mac pointed out Ira to her and she giggled.

Mac went on talking about his own life and Joy listened without paying full attention. "So, Joy," Mac purred, "how long are you going to be in town?"

With a jolt, she realized that he was staring straight down into her cleavage. A jerk, that's what he was. Had been a jerk in school, was still a jerk, would be a jerk in twenty years. She could almost hear her mother's retort. *"Do you think a woman wears a dress like that so she'll be ignored?"*

"I expect I'll be fairly busy," she answered.

"That's right. You're making an appearance at the mall." He touched his necktie and looked away. "Maybe you'll have time for dinner with an old friend?"

She couldn't believe that he was asking her for a date. Mac, who considered himself a superstud back in their own time, Mac, who commented about her weight—was asking her out.

"I don't think that I have any old friends here," she replied with delicious grandeur. She started to move away. "Pardon me now. Mustn't keep the fans waiting."

"Snob." She didn't turn back.

She spoke briefly to the others in her Health class, except for one person she didn't see. Signed more autographs. It was kind of neat, also kind of not. Every time she moved, several fans gathered around. They hung on her every word, laughed at everything she said. But they were all strangers to Joy, and she knew that she was really a stranger to them. "Do you know where the phones are?" she asked when there was a pause. "I'd like to phone my mother."

"Your mother?" The former school principal looked surprised. "Isn't she on that island you bought near Australia? I'm sure that I heard something about you buying your mother an island so she wouldn't tempt you by cooking the old family specialties. Frankly, I think she sounds very sweet."

Joy wanted to go back. She wanted to see her mother. She didn't know what she had to do to leave. "I want to go home."

The woman looked alarmed. "You still have to make a speech. Everyone is expecting it."

The room began to fade.

"Ciao," Joy called to her.

"Time to wake up," Karen said. "Open your eyes slowly. I won't turn the lights up immediately."

The room was still dark, but not as dark as it had been. The chair was upright again.

"Do you know where you are?"

" . . Night Room?"

"Tell me what year this is." Karen waited. "You'll have to speak up a little."

Joy told her the year.

Karen removed the straps and helped her to sit up. "Are you thirsty? Would you like something to drink?"

"Yes. Please." She looked down at a body with ordinary-sized breasts and extra weight because she was big boned.

"I'll bring some water. Just sip it. Then you can go out and sit with your friends. It's not a good idea to drive away immediately. Like giving blood, you know?"

Joy looked around at the blackness surrounding her as the assistant went out into the hall. The lights had come up to almost ordinary level.

A room, that's all it was. An ordinary room

3

"Joy should be back fairly soon." Barbara was sitting next to Tess in the waiting room. "Most people are disoriented for a few minutes."

"Uh-huh." Tess had brought a new photography magazine with her. This was the third time that she had started the same article, and she still had no idea whether it concerned filters or light meters.

She wanted to pace. She wanted to pace right out of the building into her car and drive home. "I don't know about this," she said for the tenth time.

Barbara gave her a reassuring smile. "You don't have to do it." She gestured for Tess to lean closer. "Was that guy hanging around again today?" she asked in a low voice.

"What guy?" Abruptly Tess realized who she meant. "Oh. No." She was sorry she'd mentioned him, even to Barbara. On the weekend someone had rung the doorbell of her house. She wouldn't have just opened the door, but Petey got there first. It had seemed straightforward enough, a wrong address . . . except that she'd seen him twice since then, at bus stops near school. He hadn't said anything either time, but she had no doubt that he recognized her. "I'm sure it was a coincidence."

"You could have an admirer," Sandra said from the next chair. "That's happened to me several times. Sometimes boys need to work up courage before they say anything. Why, just the other day—"

Tess really didn't want to hear about Sandra's social life. She stood up. "I'm going out for some air."

"Don't go far," Ms. Ruddley called.

In the cold night air, her breath plumed out as though she were a frightened dragon. Tess had her car keys in her hand, but then she dropped them back into her pocket. No, she wouldn't run away. She also wouldn't go into the Night Room.

She retraced her steps. She was about to go into the waiting room, when she spotted Karen heading down the side hallway with a paper cup in her hand. "Excuse me," she called, starting after her.

The young assistant disappeared through the door. Tess looked around. Near the entrance to the Night Room was another door she had noticed when they were given the guided tour. PRIVATE was written on the outside in large letters. It stood slightly ajar.

She moved closer. Inside the dimly lit narrow room she saw a woman with short-cropped silver hair sitting before a long control panel. Tess felt like Dorothy in *The Wizard of Oz* when she spied the wizard. *Pay no attention to that man behind the curtain.*

The woman was skimming the local newspaper, her eyeglasses pushed forward on her nose. Tess could hear voices so soft that at first she wasn't sure where the sound came from.

"It was like nothing I expected." Joy was laughing. "I mean it was so . . ."

The woman paid no attention. A wooden cane rested against one side of the console. Beyond her, Tess could see into the Night Room itself. Joy looked wiped out and more than a little giggly.

Abruptly the woman noticed her. Dr. Halstrom sat up straight, flipping a switch so the voices ceased altogether. Laying her eyeglasses to one side, she rose slowly.

"The door was open," Tess said.

"The door says PRIVATE, does it not?" The woman spoke with a harsh accent.

"Dr. Halstrom?" Tess took a step forward. Beyond the wall, Joy was trying to drink from the paper cup, her hands shaking. "I'm Tess Norville," Tess said hurriedly. "I'm with the group from Banting, and I wanted to say that I've changed my mind. I don't want to take my turn with Argus. It's nothing against the program. It's just—" She wanted to explain that she had been feeling apprehensive about taking part. If she was lucky, the scientist might have something to say about that, a comment she could use.

"Never mind." The woman turned back toward the console. "Norville." Still standing, she punched a few buttons on the keyboard. "You are removed. Now leave."

"Just like that?"

Her short bark of laughter ended in a smoker's cough. "Of course, just like that. There were seven students for tonight. You were number six. Now you are not. Did you expect a funeral oratorio each time a deletion is made? Young lady, I am working. Someday you may understand about work."

There was no *someday* about it. Tess understood about work now. "I'm with the school paper. *The Banner*. I was wondering if I could make an appointment to interview you." Dr. Halstrom had already turned down her telephone request for an interview.

"Absolutely not. You will leave this office now or I ring for the security guards. *Now,* young lady."

She left. Quickly.

As she came back into the waiting room, Barbara looked at her questioningly. Tess nodded and received a reassuring smile in return. The others were much as she had left them. Ira was doing homework, Sandra flipping through a women's magazine from the pile. Ms. Ruddley sat behind a desk, writing in a notebook. Graham was looking through the toy box in the corner.

Only Mac was in motion, pacing the room. "Did you get lost?" he asked her.

"I dropped out." The words seemed foreign. The others looked up. "I told Dr. Halstrom I didn't want to take part."

"Why?" Ira asked flatly.

"She doesn't have to give an explanation," Ms. Ruddley said.

"That's all right," Tess said. "The thing is that I know I'm going to be a reporter. So either Argus would tell me what I already know, or I'd end up arguing with the results."

"Someday I'd like to see something you didn't argue with," Ira said.

Tess's heart sank. Was he still mad because she called him Ichabod? She had always thought that Ichabod Crane in the Disney cartoon was sort of cute.

"Chicken." Mac began to cluck softly.

Tess scowled at him. "I'm not a coward."

To her surprise, he stopped. He glanced uneasily at the hallway, then back at her. "No, you're not."

"I don't need permission from you," she snapped before she could stop herself. She turned toward Ira. "Or you."

"Tess," Ms. Ruddley chided. "Learn to stop while you're ahead."

Ira seemed to be trying not to laugh. Then he winked at her. Ira actually winked at her.

Tess had the kind of feeling in her stomach that she got when she rode an unfamiliar roller coaster. "Do you have something in your eye?" she asked him.

The tall, thin boy leaned back and his chair creaked. He examined her. "Learn to stop," he droned, "when you're ahead."

"I'll remember that next time I'm in a game." Mac's chuckle seemed forced. "I'll tell Coach that Ms. Ruddley says to quit when I'm ahead. It's a new kind of strategy."

The counselor's eyes were fixed on Tess's face. "You spoke with Dr. Halstrom?"

Tess described the scientist. "She has an office next to the Night Room. The door was open. I only talked to her for a minute. I asked her for an interview, but she said no."

She had researched the reclusive scientist. At one time, Ursula Halstrom had been a champion skier. She had retired from competition after suffering severe injuries in an avalanche that killed her fiancé. Tess had also found out about Halstrom's parents. Both were noted in their fields, her mother as a psychiatrist and her father as a pioneer in computer research. Dr. Halstrom had combined both sides when she began working on the Argus project in her mid-twenties. She was now fifty-four, although she looked older.

"She doesn't give many interviews," Ms. Ruddley said sympathetically. "There are some really friendly types who are always ready to leap into your lap and lick your face. Dr. Halstrom is definitely not one of those."

Joy came through the door accompanied by Karen. Tess saw a few spots on her chest as though she'd spilled water on herself.

"So how was it?" Mac demanded.

Joy forced a smile. "Good. It was good. I'm really tired, though. It gives you a lot to think about." She went to the coatrack, but she seemed to have difficulty remembering which coat was hers.

Ms. Ruddley went up to her. "You're not driving, are you?"

She shook her head. "I'm going to call my mom."

"There's a pay phone near the washrooms," Karen said.

"Do you want to talk for a bit?" Ms. Ruddley asked.

"Maybe at school. Later."

"Joy." Tess had opened her notebook to a blank page. "The readers of the *Banner* will be curious about—"

"No comment." Joy cut her off in midsentence.

Ms. Ruddley gave her a warning look. "Tess, not now."

"Another time." Joy seemed to stand taller than usual as she wound her long scarf around her neck. "We'll do lunch."

The others traded glances as she left the room.

"Karen." Tess approached the assistant. "I'm on the school paper. I'd like to interview you about the Argus program."

The young woman looked worried. "I'll have to ask Dr. Halstrom. Leave your card and I'll get back to you."

Like high school students had business cards. Maybe she should get some printed up.

T. E. Norville
Reporter

"I'm not carrying any cards tonight. But I can leave you my phone number. Or I'll call you."

Karen wrote Tess's telephone number on the clipboard she was holding, then scanned the top page. "Okay," she said, raising her voice. "I imagine you know that one person has decided not to take part in the project. I want to ask Sandra Wilcox if she wouldn't mind rescheduling to Monday afternoon. Dr. Halstrom is speaking at a conference this weekend, and she needs additional time to prepare her presentation." She looked around. "Sandra?"

"Monday would be fine," Sandra said.

Ms. Ruddley frowned "I may not be available on Monday."

"So you should stick around," Ira told Sandra. "They didn't say that they can't handle your turn tonight."

"I honestly don't think that Argus is likely to tell me anything upsetting, Ms. Ruddley." Sandra began gathering her books. "You don't have to be there."

"MacDonald Collier," Karen called.

Mac winced.

"Mac," he said. "Just call me Mac."

* *
*
* *
4
*

"Do I have time to go, like . . ." Mac pointed toward the door leading to the hall. To the john.

"We'd prefer that you did," Karen said.

He hesitated near the door. "Don't give away my place." A little quiet time first, that's what he needed. Quiet time in a place with tiles.

He would have thought that the men's at the university would have more dignity than the high school boys'. No way. Lots of reading material on the walls. After he finished what he was there to do, which took longer than usual, he went out into the hall and took a deep breath.

He turned when he heard a quiet sob. Joy stood near a bank of telephones with tears rolling down her cheeks.

Crap. He never knew what to do around crying girls, so he avoided them whenever possible. Tears were a trap.

Two years ago he had spent the entire summer with a girl before he figured out that she could turn the waterworks on and off like a tap. That's how she got her way about everything, starting from what movie they should see. She had him jumping through hoops trying to keep her from crying. After he caught on and dumped her, that was when it really became time to man the lifeboats. Her friends spread the word around that he was an insensitive jerk. Hey, why not?

Insensitive jerks had more fun.

He supposed that Joy might be another of those types born with galloping tear ducts. If so, she was wasting her tears on an empty hall and a row of telephones. He went over to her, unsure of what to say. "Uh . . . wasn't your mother home?"

She nodded. "She'll be here soon." Joy seemed to be trying to smile through her tears, but then she gave it up. "I'm all right. Really."

Jeez. "You don't exactly look all right."

"I don't cry pretty. My sister, does, though. You should see her." She made it sound like crying was a competition event in her family.

He was supposed to be inside with the others. People were waiting for him. "Was it, like, bad for you in the Night Room?"

Joy shook her head. "Not bad." The tears were starting to well up again. She dug into her purse for a tissue. "I mean, it was and it wasn't. That's what I have to think about. And whether I can get to where I was. Or if I even want to."

Joy definitely wasn't a pretty crier. Her cheeks were red and blotchy. In combination with that orange sweat suit, her face looked like hell. He wished that somebody else would come out. "Maybe you should talk to Ms. Ruddley. That's what she's here for."

She shook her head. "I saw you at the reunion party."

"Yeah?" Maybe he could cheer her up a little. "Let me guess. Eleven years from now, I'm still mouthing off."

She didn't tell him that he was dead wrong. Great.

He really did have to go back. "Is one of the other girls a friend of yours?" Then he remembered that Tess and Sandra had left. The only girl remaining was Barbara. He didn't think that Joy was the type of girl Barbara would hang out with. "What about Ira or Graham? Do you know them?" He thought that Joy was fairly new to the school.

Joy shook her head. "I'm okay. Really."

He began to move away.

"Thanks, Mac," she called.

He just waved. She had thanked him. For what? He'd said she looked like a pumpkin.

Inside the waiting room, he shot off his big mouth again. He told Ms. Ruddley about Joy weeping in the hallway. She headed straight out. He went to join Dr. Halstrom's assistant with a clear conscience. Now he deserved a good future.

Why did he feel like God had developed Argus?

"Are we ready?" Karen asked him with a bored expression.

"We are." As he followed Karen down the hall, he felt like a Roman gladiator marching out to meet a lion.

No. He frowned. The ones who met the lions were Christians. And none of them came out alive.

"You're in luck," he said to Karen as he took off his shoes outside the Night Room. "I changed my socks this morning."

"Uh-huh."

He put on the pair of one-size-fits-all hospital booties that she handed him. "So what happens next?"

"You go into the Night Room and you sit in the chair. And I strap you in. Look, no smart cracks, all right? That's not what I get paid for. Perhaps I should mention that I have a black belt in karate. I don't want any trouble from you."

She probably looked really pretty in her karate outfit. "What do you get paid for?" he asked as he followed her into the room. "That's not a smart crack. It's a question."

"I am Dr. Halstrom's assistant."

"Which means what?" He got into the chair. The booties felt like duck feet.

"I assist her." She leaned closer as she fastened the strap across his chest. Her voice was low. "You do realize that we're under observation."

He hadn't. "Sure."

"All right. Well, I keep very busy because we have a great deal of data to process. I liaise with the schools and with the graduate students conducting the interviews."

He had been interviewed by a male student who was another Rams fan. They'd gotten along great. "So you keep churning 'em in and out."

She didn't answer.

"Doc—are you a doctor, too?"

"I'm writing my thesis. I hope to have my doctorate in another year, knock wood." She looked around as though she were trying to find a piece of wood. Lots of luck. She turned back. "Are you comfortable?"

He was comfortable, and the lights were beginning to dim. Before Mac left the waiting area, Graham had dug out a teddy bear from the toy box. Mac wished that he had it with him. Or that Karen would stay there and hold his hand. Anything.

She had gone behind the chair where he couldn't see her. A drawer opened. "Hey, Karen," he called. "What's the worst thing that ever happened to anybody in here?"

The drawer closed. She came back carrying some kind of blue headgear. "The worst thing?"

"Yeah. No kidding."

Really no kidding. This Argus thing was scaring the crap out of him.

She fastened the helmet onto his head. Mac couldn't think of any games being played that night, but somewhere nearby somebody was listening to a broadcast. He heard the unmistakable cries of a crowd cheering. Clamoring for action.

"Oh," she said, "I suppose that the worst thing was when some bad little boy didn't get his wish."

5

"Sir?"

Once, when Mac was five—before his mom split—she

had taken him to a wedding held in the banquet room of a hotel. The room in which he now found himself seemed to have twice as many people crammed together under chandeliers, laughing and talking.

Someone touched his sleeve, and he turned. His eyes widened at the sight of the waitress. Very nice. She had long honey-colored hair tied back in a ponytail. *Very.* "Your drink," she said.

He was about to search for the phony ID in his wallet, even though she hadn't asked to see it. Then he remembered. He was legal. "How much?" he asked.

She told him, and he drew in his breath. For that amount, he could buy an entire case. His breath lodged somewhere near his backbone when he caught sight of the contents of his wallet. He wasn't exactly poor. Maybe he was rich.

"Is anything wrong?" she asked.

"No." He handed her a bill, then flashed her a grin as he took his beer and removed the plastic cup placed over the top. "Keep the change."

"Thank *you,*" she said.

The beer was imported. He'd definitely moved up in the world.

Mac looked around. One reason the hall looked so big was that the walls were mirrored. He headed toward the nearest to check out his reflection. He approached himself from the front, looked himself up and down. Turned to one side. The other. Peered over his shoulder at his rear.

Whew.

He looked good! Really good. Good suit. Good hair. Some guys in the room already had bellies crowding out their belts. Not him. He was still a lean mean lovin' machine.

Karen had said he couldn't leave the hotel, but she didn't say he couldn't explore the rest of it. Maybe he had a room there. Maybe he'd see what the waitress was doing later.

"Good old Mac." He didn't hear Ira come up behind him. "Still admiring yourself."

Mac turned. He started laughing at the sight of the eleven-years-older Ira. "Jeez, man. I mean, jeez."

"Cute. Very cute." Ira feinted a jab toward his midsection, which Mac easily fended off.

"The beer," Mac said, holding out his other hand. "Watch the beer."

"At these prices, they must store the beer in a vault. Inflation is one thing. This is ridiculous." Ira sighed. "Still, it's only every ten years, right?"

Did Ira remember how old they really were? "I feel like I'm still sixteen," he said. He waited for Ira to say *Hey, we are really sixteen.*

"Not me." Ira shook his head. "I wouldn't want to be a teenager again. Do you remember dating? Wondering what you were going to say when a girl answered the phone?" He cringed, then laughed. "That's right—you're not married."

Mac gave his best wolfish grin. "How did you know?"

Ira gestured toward the other side of the room, where a crowd was milling around at a long bulletin board set up along one wall. Tess was among them, her hair put up in a twist. "Everybody's particulars are up on the board over there. High school pictures beside current ones."

"Yeah?" Maybe he'd go look at them. Mac took a long swig of his beer. It sure went down like real beer.

The waitress was crossing in his direction again. As she passed, she flashed him a smile.

"Not bad," Ira said. "But don't tell my wife I said so."

"The old ball and chain," Mac said, pitying him. The guy even wore a wedding band.

To his surprise, Ira regarded him as though the pity was mutual. "You don't know what you're missing."

Maybe not, but he sure knew what Ira was missing. "Do you remember Argus?" Mac asked.

"Who?"

"Never mind. Hey," he said, "I think I see somebody I want to talk to over there."

"Well, come on to our table later."

Maybe he should check out the bulletin board so he'd know what he had supposedly been doing for the past eleven years. He spotted Barbara sitting on a couch over to the side. He started to head over in her direction.

"I know you," a male voice said. "You played in the Fruit Bowl. Mac Collier."

He stopped as a surge of relief passed through him. He had been starting to think he'd imagined that scout looking him over. So, he made it in sports. He'd played in the Fruit Bowl. From the other man's awed tone, the accomplishment was a lot more impressive than playing in his bath water. "That's me," he said modestly. He had no idea who he was talking to.

"Too bad about your knees. I understand you run a sporting goods store now."

Crap. Still, he seemed to be doing okay.

"It must have been great for a while, earning the big bucks. All those girls coming after you."

The waitress was watching him. "They're still coming after me," he said.

That earned him a hard jab to his shoulder. He jabbed back, laughing, and the other man staggered. "What about you?" Mac asked. "What have you been up to?"

"Stock market. Doing great." He leaned closer. "I saw you drive up in a brand-new Cherry Tomato. So you can't be doing that badly yourself."

The keys to a brand-new Cherry Tomato were jingling in his pocket. Mac was fit. He looked good. His chest began to swell with pride.

Abruptly he focused in. The other man was saying something about investments. Something about buying bananas because they were sure to split. "Hey, no," Mac protested. He wasn't about to get roped into a conversation with somebody wanting to sell him stock. "Not now. I'm here to catch up on old times."

"My card," the man said. "Take my card."

Across the floor, a woman in a revealing blue dress was assessing him with a cool expression. He started to move toward her just as two women approached. She began signing autographs. Maybe he had once had a class with her. Not important. His chances were a whole lot better with the waitress.

Tess was coming his way. He put out a hand to stop her. "Hey, Tess," he said. "You're looking good." She was, definitely. Now that he saw her in a form-fitting purple dress, he could see that she was one girl he shouldn't have overlooked in high school.

At first the redhead didn't seem to recognize him. "You played football," she said.

"Mac Collier." He wondered if he could impress her with his great memory. "You were on the high school paper. You were editor." That hadn't happened yet, but everybody knew it would.

That made her smile. "Are you here with your wife?"

She wanted to know if he was married. Nobody asked him that in high school. Eleven years later was a totally different ball game. "Not me. I'm not married."

Tess probably had a room in the hotel, too. Back in his own time, Tess Norville was even real. This was kinky.

She laughed. "Some things never change."

"Can I buy you a drink?"

He could see her scanning the room again. Abruptly she frowned. "Not now. I want to talk to Graham." She moved away. "Maybe I'll take you up on that drink later. We'll get caught up on old times."

Mac stood there grinning. The waitress was looking his way again. He raised his hand slightly. She smiled and headed in his direction. He no longer had any doubts. A wonderful future lay before him.

Then he remembered one face he hadn't seen. The one female he'd sworn he'd find: Sandy Wilcox.

Mac still hadn't made it to the bulletin board. He scanned the room as he made idle conversation with some of his other former classmates, and ordered another beer from the waitress, who told him that her name was Delores.

Delores did not wear a wedding ring. As she handed him his beer, her long, slim fingers brushed his. She seemed impressed when he told her he had a brand-new Cherry Tomato. She hadn't taken a drive in one. Yet.

The woman in the low-cut blue dress turned out not to be as inviting as she looked. Apparently some girl in his class had become a stuck-up actress. That was okay. He was having a great time. Now . . . if he could just find Sandy.

He joined the others at the bulletin board. The cheat sheets were alphabetical, going from left to right and then starting over again at the far left. So he didn't see Sandra's name immediately. Then he stared. Her sheet only had a single picture, from high school. Under her name was a single word:

DECEASED

And the year she died.

"Time to wake up," Karen said.

"No, wait," Mac protested. "I have to find out something."

"Sorry." She didn't sound sorry. "Your turn is over."

He was back in the Night Room.

*
    *   *

    *   *

            6   *

"So, how did it go?" Ira asked Mac. The counselor still hadn't returned to the waiting room.

The larger boy sank onto a chair and looked around slowly. "Where's Sandra?"

"She left before you went in," Graham reminded him.

"Oh, yeah. Right." Mac closed his eyes. "Jeez." He opened his eyes again and looked at his watch. "What's the date?"

The others exchanged glances. "December seventh," Ira answered. "Thursday. The same as when you left."

"I know, but it can't have been only a half hour since I left here. That would mean I was under, like, fifteen minutes."

"It's like a dream," Barbara explained gently. "Years can pass overnight."

"Where's Tess?" Mac asked. He answered his own question. "She left, too."

"Ms. Ruddley is still with Joy," Barbara said. "I don't think she expected you out so soon."

"Believe me," Mac said, "it wasn't my idea. I was having a good time." He stretched. "I looked good. Really good." He glanced toward Ira. "Sorry about you."

"What about me?"

"Mac—" Barbara's tone was warning.

"Forget that. There was something about Sandra." Mac looked troubled. "Something weird."

"You're not supposed to say what you learned before the others go in," Barbara said. "You might taint our impressions."

"Yeah, but this is important." He fell silent.

No one said anything for a minute. "I'm next," Barbara said. "I'm not nervous, really." She turned to Ira. "Do I look nervous?"

"No more than anyone else."

"My interviewer was such a Twinkie." She stood. "Maybe I'd better use the washroom first."

"*What in hell is the Fruit Bowl?*" Mac's bellow caught them unawares. "*They said I played in the Fruit Bowl.*" He started laughing. "Man, this is weird."

Ira waited until the door closed behind Barbara. Graham still sat near the box of toys. Other than that, he and Mac were alone. "So how was it really?" he asked.

"Grown women," Mac began, "are a whole different story from girls." He stopped. "Like, this stuff isn't true, right?"

"It could be."

The laughter faded from Mac's eyes. "Do you remember how I said I was going to look up Sandra at the party? I looked for her, all right." Mac rubbed his jaw. "She was dead. She died back in high school."

Graham drew in his breath sharply.

"It was on a bulletin board. I saw her picture like she is now, only her write-up said she died this year." He looked around. "This is *December*. The year's almost up."

Fury and sickness hit Ira's stomach at the same instant. He thought he'd been successful at keeping his feelings about Sandra secret. "You always did have a crappy sense of humor," he said through gritted teeth.

Mac stood and glowered down at him. "You think I'd joke about something like that?"

Barbara came back from the washroom. She joined Graham by the toy box. "I spotted Dr. Halstrom taking a cigarette break outside. Smoking isn't allowed in the building. From what I understand, she usually goes out after every two students."

Ira barely heard her words. "I'm telling you," Mac said. "That's what I saw."

Ira had expected Mac to brag about a sexual conquest. This was even sicker. "Barb," he called. "There's something I want you to check on when you're taking your turn."

"What?" She turned with a rag doll in her arms.

"Sandy Wilcox," Ira said.

The girl groaned. "What makes her so popular? I mean, good looks and a great personality can't be everything." Barbara often bemoaned the fact that all her social invitations came from college students, who seemed too experienced for her. At the same time, her brains intimidated high school guys.

"Mac seems to think that she's—" He stopped.

"Dead," Mac intoned.

She clutched the doll to her chest. "What?"

Now Mac was pacing, too. "Maybe I made a mistake. Maybe it was somebody else." He stopped. "There's a bulletin board along one wall. Everybody else had two pictures. She had one. It was her." He sat again, looking around. "Has Tess definitely dropped out? She could get to the bottom of this in a minute."

"Tess said that Dr. Halstrom pressed a button on the computer," Graham answered. "She's out."

"I saw Tess in the future," Mac said. "She looked pretty good. No kidding. There's more to this girl than she lets on."

In another second Mac would probably claim he'd successfully hit on Tess. Or she'd hit on him. Ira was beginning to feel violent again. Then he realized something illogical about Mac's report. "Wait!" he yelled. "If Tess had already dropped out, why would you see her at all?"

Mac's head went up. "Right. She shouldn't be there."

"Yes, she should," Barbara answered. "As background. Tess went through the interviews, so it would be surprising if she *weren't* there. The part that doesn't make sense is the date. Argus shouldn't provide hard information about an event that hasn't occurred."

"Everything else at the party made sense." Mac looked at Ira. "There was this little waitress. Man, when I left the party, things were getting close."

The door opened.

"Barbara Flores," Karen called.

"This," Barbara said, "is going to be so strange."

7

"Argus was named after a dog, you know," Barbara said as Karen brought out the helmet.

"I know." Karen slipped the unit over her head, and Barbara tried to relax. The chair felt huge to her.

The dog Argus was special, right up there with Lassie and Benji. The Argus in *The Odyssey* was known for his memory, recognizing his former master, the Greek hero Odysseus, after the man had been away at war for more than a decade. That was the purpose of the computer-generated Argus, to "remember" them in the future, projecting patterns that might span the years.

In her case, Barbara wasn't convinced that the pup had been introduced to even the slightest semblance of the real Barbara. She was even more skeptical now, after hearing about Sandra's supposed nonfuture.

"I'm not so sure about the information my interviewer gave to Argus," she said to Karen. "It might not be valid."

"No?"

"She seemed distracted."

Distracted didn't cover the situation. Her interviewer had been in the middle of a phone argument with her boy-friend. Every time Barbara started to answer a question, the phone would ring again. The young woman would stop writing, continue her quarrel, then slam down the receiver again.

Barbara had just been starting to tell her about her plans to enter a branch of the sciences when the interviewer put down her pencil. "This won't take long." She dialed the phone, then launched into a lengthy tirade.

While she waited, Barbara had picked up a paperback that had slipped from the interviewer's briefcase. The cover showed a woman in a low-cut pink ball gown, half-reclining, auburn curls thrown back, while a man stripped to the waist seemed about to sink his teeth into her neck. The title was something like *Love's Rapturous Plunge into the Whirlpool of Desire*.

The receiver slammed down. "Now, where were we?"

"Talking about my career plans," Barbara reminded her.

"No, I believe we covered that. Let's go on to romance."

As Barbara winced, the phone rang again.

The ceiling had darkened to a semblance of the evening sky. "I'm not sure how valid this is likely to be," she murmured. Nice doggy. Good Argus.

"Most people find something to think about." Karen stepped back. "Are you comfortable?"

Barbara was comfortable. "Too bad," she said. The sky was becoming inky. "Too bad."

"Too bad about what?" Karen asked at the door.

"There's night in here . . . but no sunset." The door closed. There was no orange glow of flaming gases from 150 million kilometers away. "Night but never morning."

Barbara yawned again as the door closed. She lay there and watched the lights. From somewhere nearby she heard what sounded like the hum of a sewing machine. Whir-stop. Whir-stop.

Whirrrrrrrrrrrrrrrrrrrrrrrrrrrr.

She was sitting on a chair near a window, wearing an emerald green dress that was loose and flowing. Nearby, people were chatting, not paying any attention to her. That was good. She didn't mind starting off invisible. She looked around, trying to see whether she recognized any faces. She didn't notice the man moving to her side.

"Here you are, darling." A glass was held out in her direction. She glanced around before taking it. "They didn't have any milk at the bar, so I brought you orange juice."

Her parents always brought her juice, too, when they attended a function where liquor was served.

"Thank you." As she took the glass, she looked up and caught her breath. "Wow."

"What?" He looked around. "Did you see someone you know?"

She practically dribbled the juice down her front.

He—the man—had to be at least thirty, but he was handsomer than anyone she'd ever seen outside of a movie. Handsomer than she'd seen in most movies.

"No. I mean, the glass is cold. I mean, thank you."

"My pleasure."

He smiled. She had never seen such even white teeth. This was a man to be cloned. The strange part was that he looked vaguely familiar. She knew she had never seen him before. He had called her darling.

"Can I get you anything else, sweetheart?" he asked.

Now he had called her sweetheart.

"No, thanks. I mean, I'm okay."

She seemed to be sitting peculiarly. As she tried to straighten without spilling her juice, she couldn't help noticing that there seemed to be more of her than usual. In eleven years, she'd put on a lot of weight. Her grandmother always said she was too thin, but this was ridiculous.

"If you'll excuse me, then," the man said, "I'm off to talk football with one of your former classmates—if I can drag him away from that waitress he's following."

"Sure."

Barbara drank. Then, as she set her empty glass on a small table, something moved along her belly. She jumped.

Unbelievably, impossibly, it had moved *inside* her.

She put her hands at the sides of her abdomen. Pushed. Her abdomen pushed back. She had seen both *Alien* and *Aliens*. She knew about parasitical growths.

"Well, look at you!" It was Tess. An older Tess. A Tess who looked great.

"Look at me?" She laughed. "Look at you!"

"I'm not the one who looks like she's expecting twins."

Barbara had to hold on to the armrests to push herself out of her chair. She slowly turned toward the mirrored wall.

She wasn't fat. She was—

"You're not, are you? Expecting twins?"

—pregnant.

Wow.

"Barb?"

This was so far out. "I don't believe this," Barb breathed. "There's a human being inside me. And it moves. It—"

She had given some thought about having children in the future. Two of them. She was even toying with the idea of eventually going to a genius sperm bank. Had she?

"I introduced myself to your husband." Tess nodded toward the hunk who'd brought the juice.

Husband!

Tess waved her hand in front of her as though she was fanning herself. "I understand that Carlo was one of your models. Now that I see him, I can believe it."

One of her what? Did Tess mean that she'd built him from scratch?

No way. Barbara began to reason. Cloning started at the cell stage. This guy was older than she was. Probably not much, though. In eleven years, she'd be twenty-seven. This definitely answered one burning question from high school. At some point, she must have had a date.

"It's funny how things turn out," Tess mused. "Who could have ever predicted that you would design sportswear?"

Thud. "No one," Barbara answered flatly. "No one in the world. I would have said that I had no talent for art whatever."

"Have you *seen* Joy?" Tess didn't wait for her response. "She has certainly changed since high school. In fact, I don't see many areas that she hasn't changed. Still, you have to admit that it livens up things, having a real movie star at the party." Tess took a small notebook from her purse. "If you'll excuse me, I want to see if I can set up an interview with her."

An interview meant that Tess was associated with a newspaper. At least *something* sounded accurate.

"I loved your spring collection," a passing woman enthused.

"Thanks." Barbara gritted her teeth. A fashion designer. She wondered what on earth she had said to the Twinkie to make her think that she had any interest whatever in fashions.

Suddenly she knew why her "husband" seemed familiar. Carlo resembled the man on the cover of the book that her interviewer had been reading. She'd been handed the Twinkie's own dream man.

Her midsection was acting up again. She placed her hand flat against it, not minding the movement now that she knew what it was. She was beginning to find this pregnancy business fascinating. Her body had done this all by itself. She decided the baby was a girl. Melanie was a name she particularly liked.

The baby kicked harder. The sensation was fantastic. Now she was beginning to understand why Dr. Halstrom had spent her entire career working on Argus.

No! She brought herself back to reality sharply. This wasn't real. Her pregnancy was only an illusion. This wasn't Melanie. Her sportswear company was an illusion as well. She seldom thought about clothes. Her opinion of handsome men was that they were all conceited.

Her phantom child was a strong kicker. "Baby," she said softly to it, "this is Mommy. Things are weird. Just enjoy the orange juice for a while. I'm going to try to figure this out." She had remembered Sandra Wilcox.

As Mac had described, one wall contained updates of people in their class. She moved toward it. "Excuse me." The area was crowded. "Excuse me." The crowd glanced at her distended abdomen, then parted like the Red Sea.

"Barbara!" She turned at Mac's voice.

She stared at him. "You look good."

He grinned and turned around so she could admire his suit. "You look good, too. I mean, you're so big." He was staring at her belly. "I mean . . . wow, who would have thought?"

Not her. That was for sure. She supposed she was being rude, but she wanted to find out what she could about Sandra.

Mac's eye was roving toward a waitress. Barbara laid her hand on his sleeve. "Mac," she said, "I've been looking for Sandra Wilcox."

Abruptly she found herself with his complete attention. "I guess you forgot," he said solemnly.

"Forgot what?" She decided to feign complete ignorance. "I wondered what became of her. She was always serving on committees, and all the guys were drooling over her."

"She didn't make it to her senior year. You remember now, don't you?"

"But what happened?"

"Barbara!" her husband called. "Over here."

Mac flashed her a toothy grin. "I own some outfits that you designed. Sharp. Very sharp." He nodded toward the waitress. "Excuse me, okay? I think she's humming my tune."

He was gone. Barbara turned and found her husband near the bulletin board. She joined him near the Fs.

"This was you?" He seemed amused.

The picture wasn't one she recognized, but it was definitely her. Cute. She had been cute in high school.

Was cute.

Wasn't really pregnant.

The baby kicked her as if in protest.

"Sorry." Was. Sort of.

Her husband took both her hands and looked into her eyes. "Of course boys didn't notice you," he said in a deep, velvety voice. "Boys are stupid. They see only what is before them."

She could learn to like this guy. If she didn't watch herself, she might even start liking the Twinkie. She still couldn't figure out the part about sportswear.

"Sandra Wilcox," she said, and detached one hand. They moved along the displayed photographs, holding hands.

It was . . . nice.

"Here." Carlo stopped before the sheet of paper that held only a single photograph. DECEASED. "Was she a friend?"

Barbara shook her head, dazed. "I knew who she was. Everyone knew who she was."

Is. Back in her own time, Sandra was very much alive.

Healthy. Not merely happy but disgustingly ecstatic. Pretty. Popular. Handsome boyfriend.

"Excuse me." Barbara turned to a vaguely familiar woman. "I was trying to remember. What happened to Sandra Wilcox?"

The woman had been smiling. Her face fell. "It was all over the school. Don't you remember?"

"I must have been out with the flu when it happened," she improvised.

"Everybody talked about it for months. Her poor sisters."

"What happened to her?" Barbara ground out.

"It was so sudden. No one expected it." Her voice lowered. "She killed herself."

* * *
*
*
*

8

Michael couldn't concentrate on the image on his computer screen. He wasn't working on anything difficult, but he kept having to backtrack, to fix more mistakes. He finally decided to go downstairs and read the newspaper.

"You aren't coming down with a fever, are you, Michael?" his mother asked when he came into the living room. "I told you that you should put on a jacket when you went out this afternoon. But no, you just rushed out in a light sweatshirt—in December, for heaven's sake."

"I had to make a phone call." Immediately he realized that he should have told his mother something else. His mind wasn't working right, wasn't letting him think of anything except the clock. The student group had started at five, and it was almost seven now. The program averaged half an hour for each student. Dr. Halstrom took a nicotine break after every two students.

"You went out just to make a phone call?" His mother looked at him peculiarly. "We have telephones all over the house."

He had made the call from a public phone, confirming that the scheduled session in the Night Room was going ahead. He hadn't wanted to call from home because the Finstater Foundation might keep records of incoming calls. Their records would become part of any police investigation. When the woman at the university answered, he had almost been overwhelmed by a sudden need to confess. Instead, he had pretended to be a high school student, confirming the schedule.

Afterward, he had walked back slowly, barely feeling the light snow that had started to come down. By the time he reached home, the thin cloth of the sweatshirt was sticking to his body. "The call was about computer stuff," he told his mother.

"Of course. Why didn't I realize that?" She was looking at him with real concern. "You're shaking. I think that we should take your temperature, just in case. Perhaps I could make you a cup of tea with honey, the way I did when you were small."

"Thanks," he said, wondering if he'd ever feel warm again. "Tea would be good."

As she headed toward the kitchen, she stopped. "Michael, have you done something wrong?"

"What?" He stared at her.

"You have this guilty look, like when you were a little boy and went into the cookie jar." Her laugh was light. "Let me guess. It has to do with computer hacking. You've broken into the Department of Defense and you're about to start a world war. Or you've uncovered the formula for Coca-Cola."

"Not exactly," he said. "Mom—"

"Don't tell me about it." She started toward the kitchen. "I don't believe I want to know."

9

Joy had talked with Ms. Ruddley for a while, and now she felt better. Her mother was supposed to drive into the parking lot, so she had gone back into the main hallway to watch for her. She was startled to see a familiar face. "Tess! I thought you left."

"I was planning to go home." The red-haired girl held up her spiral notebook. "I decided to get comments from everybody for the paper." She looked both ways with a guilty expression. "Where is Ms. Ruddley?"

"She stayed to make a phone call in the staff lounge."

Tess pulled a pen from her bag. "How did it feel to wake up in the future?"

"I didn't recognize myself," Joy blurted out. "I was really thin." She flushed. "Please don't put that in the newspaper."

"I'll just mention that some students found that they'd changed physically." Tess paused. "Did you enjoy yourself?"

"Some of the time. Some of it, not at all. It was strange seeing the others in the class, only older."

"Did you see me?" Tess fumbled with her notebook and almost dropped it. "I can't believe I asked that. Please don't answer."

"But—"

"Really, I don't want to know. I'd like to hear whether you felt the program had value for you."

Joy spotted car lights outside. "Another time, okay? That's my mom." She pulled on her gloves and hurried out.

"You look flushed," Mrs. Abercrombie said as her daughter slid into the car. "You haven't been crying, have you?"

"The cold weather makes my eyes run." Joy grabbed a tissue from the box on the dashboard. "And my nose." She felt better after talking with Ms. Ruddley, but that didn't mean she wanted to discuss her experience with her mother. Not yet, anyway.

"Well, buckle up." Her mother pulled out. "So, did you see yourself as a secretary?"

"Ms. Ruddley says that if we're to get the maximum value from Argus, we shouldn't discuss it with anybody for a few days. Otherwise we're likely to focus on some parts and forget others."

Mrs. Abercrombie pressed her lips together. "None of my business, you mean."

"I'll tell you everything in a few days, all right?"

At last her mother nodded. "Fair enough. As long as you don't shut me out totally."

They drove along in silence. After they reached the shops, Christmas lights shone on either side. Scenes from the party kept whirling through Joy's head. In the future she had been perfect, and yet nothing had changed.

"Maybe I'll go to that caroling practice after all," she said.

Her mother abruptly swerved in traffic. "Next time," she said as she steadied the car, "next time you agree with me, I want advance warning."

* * *
*   *
10   *

When Tess returned to the waiting area, Barbara had just returned from the Night Room. She looked exhausted. Mac and Ira were sitting close to her. Graham was still holding a teddy bear. "I thought you went home," Ira said.

"I'm with the school paper, remember?" she replied breezily. "I want to interview the survivors."

She was startled by the sharp look Ira gave her as he stood. "What do you know?" he asked. He seemed taller, more imposing.

"What?" Her reporter's nose for news began to itch. "Did something happen to someone in there?"

Surely not. She had been directly outside in the hallway. No ambulances could have sneaked by her. She wasn't even sure whether Argus could injure someone, although the resuscitation equipment in the Night Room certainly made it look as though the possibility existed.

"Everybody's fine," Mac said easily. Too easily. "Doesn't everybody look fine?"

No. They didn't. Barbara and Mac had bleary expressions as though they had been up all night. Graham looked just plain worried.

Later. Barbara mouthed the word at her.

"Mac." Tess turned to him. "Let's talk about the future."

"Okay." He seemed to be staring at her chest.

Tess glanced down. She was still wearing her khaki shirt. "What?"

Mac managed to tear his attention away to look at her face. His knowing grin seemed almost normal. "You want to know what happens between us in the future. Like in the elevator?"

"Nothing happens in the elevator," Tess said. "I wouldn't even get into an elevator with you."

"Okay," Mac said after a moment. "Then, you want to know what happens between us on the stairs?"

"No elevator," Tess said. "No stairs. I'd rather jump out the window." Ira laughed. "And I really would like to hear about your experiences."

"I'm sure that Mac would like to tell you how good he looked." Barb's hand was resting on her abdomen, and Tess wondered if she had a stomachache.

She opened her notebook to a fresh page. "Yes, Mac. Please tell your fellow students how good you looked."

That seemed to interest him. "I looked really good."

Ira was staring toward the hallway as though he could see into the Night Room itself.

Tess's nose itched like crazy. Something was definitely going on that the others didn't want her to know about.

The door opened. "Graham Hork," Karen called.

"Remember," Ira said to him.

Graham nodded. "I will." He turned toward the others. "Well . . . " He handed the teddy bear to Tess like a runner passing a baton. "See you."

"See you," she said. "Hey—good luck."

* *
*
*
11 *
*

Graham had a hole in one sock. It was so big that almost his entire big toe went through. He put on the hospital slippers as fast as he could. Karen saw, though. He was almost positive.

She was almost too polite to him, with the kind of courtesy people had when they wished you'd take your business someplace else. Her voice was flat as she gestured toward the chair. "Just sit down. Your arms should go on the rests."

"I can tell that much." He could also tell that she thought he was stupid. Graham sat gingerly in the chair, feeling like he was about to get his teeth drilled. "I guess you're more used to people from the college coming through here."

"You're right." She seemed almost embarrassed for a moment. "Actually, yours is only the third high school class."

"In the whole world?"

The expression returned to her eyes, the one that said he was dumb. "The Finstater Foundation has its quarters at this campus."

Ms. Ruddley had told them about the research outfit behind Argus. Some rich man died whom Dr. Halstrom had planned to marry. Lucky for her, he guessed, unless maybe she liked the guy.

Karen fastened the straps around him. He didn't care for that. "These are so I don't fall down, right?"

"Right. You can release yourself at any time after you come to full consciousness. It isn't difficult."

His bonds were fiddly, maybe, but not hard to unfasten. Graham had been told by more than one teacher that he had good mechanical ability. (Not the ones who taught English or History. No way. They only cared about that kind of thing when their cars or their VCRs broke down. Then they were like turtles turned onto their backs.)

"It looks something like a bicycle helmet," he said when she brought out Argus. Not regulation, though. It didn't look like it would provide much protection in an accident.

She sighed, then went around to where he couldn't see her. "Are you comfortable?"

Snug as a bug in a rug. "Sure." Except that he didn't like straps holding him down like he was a crazy person. More straps as she fastened the helmet.

"I'm leaving the room now," Karen said. "Just watch the lights as they come on. Glance around the room until you find one that sings to you."

A light that sings. Sure.

Mindful that people were waiting for him to get through his turn, Graham found a small pale blue light that seemed like it probably wouldn't get much attention in this lifetime.

He concentrated on that.

He heard the tinkling of ice cubes. Felt the crowd before he saw it. "What do you think?" Mac asked next to him. "The waitress. You had to see that look she just gave me."

Graham turned. He was at a party, just like Ms. Ruddley said. He was—no fooling—standing at a crowded bar. Somewhere behind him, music played softly—current stuff except not the way it was usually played. And Mac was there, but he'd changed. His hair was different and everything. Graham looked down at himself. He was wearing some kind of jacket. Son of a gun. Maybe he was a little dizzy, but he'd made it.

"Hey, Graham." Mac snapped his fingers before his eyes. "Are you in a coma or something? You can't be that juiced unless you had a head start before you got here."

"Wha' mean?" Graham tried to form the words, but his tongue wouldn't obey him. He had an awful taste in his mouth. He tried to focus on Mac. "You're older," he managed, and then giggled.

"Speak for yourself, buddy." Mac slapped him on the shoulder.

For some reason, the whole thing struck Graham as funny. Funny as hell. He began laughing. Around him, people turned.

After a second, Mac joined in. He stopped laughing before Graham. "Jeez." Mac gestured toward an empty glass on the bar. "Did you make it through that one already? Maybe you'd better slow down. Otherwise you're likely to miss the presentations."

Graham stared at the ice cubes melting in the glass before him, and recoiled. "I don't drink," he whispered.

He didn't. He swore that he'd never. Swore on his grandma's Bible.

"Maybe you shouldn't drink," Mac said. "But it looks like

you've had plenty of practice." He slapped Graham's shoulder again, this time more lightly. "Excuse me. I think someone is trying to move in on my territory." He walked away toward the waitress.

Graham didn't register the bartender standing before him. "Another of the same, sir?"

"No." Graham shook his head. His head felt like it was corkscrewing around. "No, I don't drink."

The bartender threw him a skeptical glance as he cleared away the empty glass. Graham walked away from the bar. Ira—the others—had asked him to find out something.

Sandra Wilcox. Right. Like he'd been told, a bulletin board was set up along one wall. He aimed himself and headed toward it.

This was all wrong. Everything seemed out of kilter, skewed. He had to walk carefully to cross the room. Even then, he jostled a woman's arm when he thought he wasn't anywhere near her. He ended up muttering that he was sorry after he was long past.

He was heading toward Wilcox, but somehow he ended up before his own name. GRAHAM HORK. That was him. The bottom picture was him. He didn't know about the top one except that it looked something like his uncle Dennis, who he was supposed to resemble. He had no idea why they'd put up a picture of his uncle Dennis. Maybe it was supposed to be funny.

He thought it was funny.

The print was swimming before his eyes, so he leaned closer to get a look at what the people from the reunion committee said about him. OCCUPATION: ODD JOBS.

THURSDAY, DECEMBER 7

"No way!" Graham said loudly. "No. Way." No way was he going to spend his life doing bits and pieces. He wasn't sure what he was going to do, except that it would be steady. He looked again. MARRIED.

His uncle Dennis wasn't married, although he had been living with a woman for two years—a record for him. Maybe his uncle Dennis had decided to get married.

"Oh, Graham," came a female's whiny voice, "you said you'd only have one."

He turned slowly to face a skinny, frizzy-haired woman in a flowered party dress that was too big for her. Didn't look crisp like the others in the room, either. Graham pointed toward himself. "You talking to me?"

"Oh, Graham," she said again.

He was supposed to be finding out about Sandra Wilcox, not talking to somebody who maybe remembered him from some long-ago History class. "This is some party, huh?" He tried to be polite. "Well, see you later."

She blocked his way. "Please stop walking away. I'm your wife. Introduce me to your old friends."

Right at that moment he couldn't have walked away from her if he was paid. The room had mirrors everywhere he looked. With a sinking feeling, he turned until he found himself facing his uncle Dennis. He looked at the bulletin board again. It was him. "Hey," he said weakly. "Hey."

"How much?" she demanded quietly. "How much did you have?"

"One," he said. One that he knew of. "I don't know." He found himself getting angry. Is this what he'd done with his life? Saddled himself with a skinny nag? The woman didn't have much more in front than she had in back. He wondered what she'd done to get him to marry her.

Looked at the bulletin board. CHILDREN: NONE

That didn't surprise him one bit, with her being so skinny and all. He looked back into her eyes. Saw something soft and hurt that made him feel ashamed. Angry, too. "This isn't real," he said. He thought of explaining to her about Argus.

"*How much*, Graham?" Whatever he had seen before, or thought he had seen, was replaced by a tone of long-suffering patience that, just for a second, made him feel like smacking her across the face.

"Back off. I can handle it." Of course he could handle it. Now that he thought about it, he was feeling pretty loose about this party. He had never liked the idea of parties before. He grabbed her arm. "Come on. Let's dance." He didn't know how to dance beyond doing the hokey-pokey. That was okay.

"Do you hear any music?" She waited. There had been a band somewhere, he was sure of it. "Oh, Graham, you promised." She put her hand on his arm. "Maybe you should go lie down in the truck for a while. If anybody asks, I'll tell the others you have a touch of the flu."

Now she was making excuses for him. He knew he had to get away from this woman. He pulled away, but she seemed attached to his arm. "Let go of me."

"Graham, no."

He realized that it probably seemed like he was heading toward the bar again, but he wasn't. The woman—this so-called wife—she was the problem.

"Graham? Graham Hork?"

"Tess?" He could have wept at the sight of a familiar face. "Tess, it's Argus. Not me." He stopped. She was exchanging uneasy glances with his wife. Not his wife. Hell, he didn't even know her name.

"It's the flu," the woman said. "He has a touch of the flu, but he really wanted to come here, to see his old friends."

"She says I'm drunk," Graham said, just to be nasty. He threw an arm around Tess's neck. "It's a party, right?"

"It is a party."

As Tess gently disengaged herself, Graham stumbled and fell against his wife. Despite her scrawniness, she managed to hold him up.

Tess smiled brightly. "I see Ira over there. Excuse me."

The woman was still holding on to him. All of a sudden Graham needed air, couldn't breathe. "Let go of me, damn it." He tried to shake her loose, but she held on with surprising strength. "Look, I'm going to the men's now. Do you go to the bathroom with me, too? Well?"

"I'll wait for you outside."

"No." He tried to pull away. "No, you will damned well not wait for me." She wanted to spy on him, make sure that he didn't have anything else to drink. Or, anyway, make sure that he didn't enjoy it. The music was playing again.

"I'll wait."

It was her. She was smothering him. He had to get away from her.

A shove. That was all he meant to do. But somehow he ended up swinging out and hitting her in the face.

She just stood there with a wounded deer look. All around them, people gaped.

"I never meant—I just wanted—" He backed away. "I didn't do that. It wasn't me." He thought he saw something else in her eyes. Triumph. His stomach was clenching and unclenching like a fist. A sour taste filled his mouth. "I need to find the bathroom." He looked around wildly, taking deep breaths. "Where's the bathroom? Please?"

Someone pointed toward the hallway. He made it just in time.

He was retching and retching.

Straps were being unbuckled. "Take it easy." Someone pushed him into a sitting position. "Steady. Don't fall."

Dry retching. He didn't know why nothing was coming out, because he'd just been drinking. He felt like his guts should be coming out.

Another woman was with her, this one older, although she let Karen do all the work.

The older woman's voice was commanding. "Take deep breaths. You are back in the Night Room. Deep breaths." He was trying. "You know where you are, yes?" She waited. "Tell me."

This was the men's room. They shouldn't be in the men's. Couldn't he get away from nagging women anywhere?

"I am speaking to you. Where are you?" He heard her muttering. "Number four. What is his first name?"

"Graham." Someone was taking some kind of blue party hat off his head.

"Graham, where are you?"

He was drenched with sweat, his fingers digging into the black padding. ". . . party." He could still hear people in the ballroom. They were talking about him.

"Does this look like a party?" Dr. Halstrom demanded. "Look around. Breathe with me. Slowly. Watch me." She raised her voice. "You will breathe in through your nose, out through your mouth. See how it is done."

His heart was trying to ram its way out of his chest. He tried breathing the way she said, but he needed all the air he could get, so he ended up gasping. "I can't."

"Do not tell me what you can't do. You can. You will."

He almost managed.

She was trying to hold a small flashlight up to his eyes. "What year is this?"

One of those teeny lights on the chandeliers was winking at him. Getting closer.

He batted it away, almost falling as he scrambled off the table. Karen tried to stop him, and he might have hit her, except that he was running out the door slipping on the floor in his hospital shoes, running to get the hell out of there.

Maybe he was drunk, but he wasn't dizzy anymore.

"Stop him!" Dr. Halstrom's voice was loud. "Stop that boy!"

12

Something was going on down the hall.

Ira was standing by the door when he heard loud voices. "What the—"

Tess dropped the magazine she was holding. "What's happening?" There was a loud thud against the outside doors.

"Stop him!" Karen appeared, disheveled. "He's heading across the field. Don't let him reach the road—a car might hit him."

"Anything you say, sweetheart." Mac was the first one out the door. All of them took off after the fleeing Graham.

Maybe he was a showoff, but Mac was also one heck of a runner. He was far ahead of the rest as they ran over a lawn of crystallized grass. Graham didn't have much of a head start. He had lost one of his booties going through the door. The other came off when Mac tackled him, along with his remaining sock.

He lay facedown, screaming and struggling, begging to be let go. Swearing. As Ira caught up, Mac was trying to hold Graham's arms behind his back. "What should I do with him?" he shouted.

"Just immobilize him." Karen sounded worried. "Don't hurt him. He should come out of it soon."

Graham was bucking like a horse. One of his arms came loose. He tried to smash Mac's face with his elbow. "Hey!" Mac yelled. "How about somebody giving me some help?"

Ira had never been in a fight in his life, not that this was one. He tried to figure out how he could best assist.

"Oh, for heaven's sake." Tess grabbed Graham's other arm and threw her weight across it. "Graham, stop it. Stop it right now." She sounded like an annoyed baby-sitter.

"You said you had a black belt!" Mac yelled at Karen.

"Well, I don't," she shouted back.

Barbara stationed herself near Graham's head. "Graham, listen to me. I don't know what you saw. But it didn't happen."

Graham seemed to be tiring. He was sobbing. At first Ira couldn't understand what he was saying.

"What, Graham?" Barbara persisted.

They all listened as he managed to get the words out. "I was there. It was real."

"I was there, too, Graham," Barbara said. "I was pregnant. Did you see me? I was huge. Look at me, Graham."

His face was ground into the grass, but she was directly in front of him.

"Graham, it was so real that I could feel the baby move. I had a husband, too." Now they were all listening.

"So what?" Graham's voice was low. "So in ten years you're having a baby."

"Graham, in ten years I might have a baby. This was just what might happen. Whatever you experienced, that *might* happen."

"What did you see?" Ira asked him.

No answer. Just that rough sobbing that seemed torn from the ground.

"Graham," Mac said, "it's got to be really uncomfortable down there. If I let you sit up, will you be okay?"

Nothing, but the struggles had stopped.

"Come on, man, it's too cold for this. I'm going to let you up. If you still want to play, I'll bring you down again. I can keep this up longer than you can. Okay?" Slowly he got off Graham, never letting his eyes stray. Tess eased up as well, but she stayed beside the downed boy.

At last Graham raised himself to a sitting position. "Did I hit you?" he asked Tess.

"You didn't hit anyone," she answered. "Not even Mac."

"You got close, though," Mac said. "You should try out for the wrestling team."

Graham was shivering violently. "I hit her." He spoke softly. "My wife." Ms. Ruddley was hurrying toward them across the lawn. "The program said I was going to be a drunk."

Barbara's voice rose. "The program doesn't know that. It only shows what might happen. Just like I might not even be able to have children."

"If I get to be like that—" The boy's voice was firmer. "If I ever treat a woman like that—if she lets me—first I'll put a gun to her head and then I'll put it to mine."

"This is one of the dangers," Tess said to Ira. She was holding Graham's hand even though he seemed unaware that she was there. "People *believe*."

Graham looked up at Ira. "Sorry, I never found out about Sandra. I was too . . ." He hung his head.

"That's okay, man."

Ms. Ruddley reached them. She squatted next to Graham. Barbara brought his sock and the bootie. The counselor helped Graham stand up. They began talking slow and steady.

Ira saw Karen starting back toward the building. He caught up with her. "It's my turn, right?"

She stopped and stared at him. "You still want to go ahead?"

"Sure."

"Your counselor might have something to say about that. She doesn't seem precisely pleased with us right now."

"I'm not Graham. Everybody else did okay. I understand that the program is educational, and I'm willing to take my chances." He kept his tone light. "My permission forms are signed. I'm not afraid. It's all programmed, right?"

"Well, yes."

Graham had run into his worst nightmare. Ira wasn't sure what his worst nightmare would be, except that having Sandy Wilcox die—for real—had become a big part of it. He had to save her.

"I'll talk to Dr. Halstrom," Karen said.

He held open the door for her. "So let's go."

13

"Dr. Halstrom says that it's all right," Karen said. "You can take your turn."

"Great." He had only been back in the waiting room for a few minutes. Everybody else was still outside with Graham. Ira looked around. It seemed weird to be sailing on to his future without anybody there to wave good-bye.

Tess came through the door. "Ms. Ruddley's talking to Graham," she told him. "He's calmer."

"Good." Ira swallowed. "Well, it's my turn. See you."

"*Are you crazy?*" Tess fairly yelled the words. "You saw what just happened to Graham. This program can hurt people."

"If you want to think about it some more—maybe talk it over with your girlfriend . . ." Karen nodded toward Tess. "Your appointment can be reset. You and Sandra Wilcox might come in together."

Sandra Wilcox was the only reason he was continuing. If what Argus foresaw was true, no one knew how much longer she had to live. Then the assistant's words hit him. "This is not my girlfriend," he said at the same time that Tess protested, "He is not my boyfriend."

Karen looked from one to the other. "I almost forgot.

You're high school students, aren't you?" He couldn't see what that had to do with anything.

"Ira," Tess said, "did you read the article I gave you?"

"Article?" At school she'd given him a photocopy of an article. He'd shoved it into his binder after giving it a scant glance. Something about holodecks. "It's at home. I'll read it later."

"Ira—"

There was an expression in the red-haired girl's eyes that he had never seen before. Real fear. For him?

"Hey," he said gently, "I'll be fine. Here." He handed her the magazine he'd been reading. "If you're around when I get out, I'll give you an interview."

Tess was looking at him and he was looking at her. Their faces seemed to be getting closer.

Karen cleared her throat. Abruptly both took a step back. "You should have read the article," Tess said soberly.

"Later." With a wink, he left her standing there.

"What article was your—what article was she referring to?" Karen asked as they walked into the Night Room. "Something about Argus?"

"I'm not sure. It's from a science fiction magazine." He didn't want to think about that now. He sat in the chair and looked around as the first strap was drawn across his chest. His earlier glimpse of the Night Room had shown him a lot of black paint and lights. It felt different now. Real, genuine night was outside the building. This was a setting for a magician.

His left foot kept twitching in its hospital shoe. He tried to keep it still. "Sorry."

"That's all right." Karen fastened a padded cuff securely around his left wrist. She went around to the other side.

"Wait," he announced suddenly.

"No problem." From her kind expression, it was obvious that she thought he had changed his mind. "After your friend's experience, I don't blame you."

"It's not that. My nose itches." In his case, that covered a lot of territory. He scratched, then put his arm down again. "Okay, now I'm fine." He was, too. He felt strangely calm. Even his toes had stopped twitching. "What now?"

She fastened the cuff. "Just lie there and familiarize yourself with your surroundings. That's what most people do."

"Why black?" he asked after a few minutes. Karen was writing on her clipboard. "Why not dark green or midnight blue?" He couldn't remember why the sky was blue. There was a reason. Something about the sun's spectrum.

"I'm really not sure."

The room seemed to be getting darker. "You're trying to turn down the lights without my noticing."

"You're welcome to notice everything that's happening. In fact, Dr. Halstrom encourages it."

He tried to remember how the adage went: *It's always darkest before it's pitch black.*

She went behind the chair and fiddled around for a while longer. A drawer opened and closed. "This is it," she said as she came around again.

"The crown," Ira said drowsily.

She fastened it on his head. "Are the straps too tight?"

" . . . 's fine."

"I'll leave you alone for a while," she said. He watched as she went out.

Sandra. He was doing this for Sandra. He lay there as the room dimmed and he was alone with the slowly moving lights. Somewhere nearby, someone was listening to a tinny radio.

He heard songs of love.

He was sitting on a bed in a hotel room, wearing a dark suit, and he wasn't alone.

A woman stood a few inches in front of him, facing away. She wore a form-fitting dress in a deep purple shade, cut low in back. High heels. Muzzily, he stared at an expanse of creamy flesh. At violet lace revealed by a zipper at half-mast.

Her shoulders were thrown back. She held out a long crystal earring that caught the light.

"Zip me up the rest of the way, will you, sweetheart?" she requested in a throaty voice.

‎ ✱ ✱
‎ ✱ ✱
‎ ✱
14 ✱

"Uh-h-h-h." He couldn't move.

The unknown woman sucked in her breath. "I haven't put on weight, have I? I couldn't have."

"No." He gulped. "You're fine."

There was laughter in her voice. "Let's go, then. The others will be wondering what's happened to us." Conscious that he was sitting on a thoroughly unmade and rumpled bed, Ira took a deep breath, then zipped the dress of a perfect stranger. (Maybe not absolutely perfect, but a whole lot better than okay.)

"Have you seen my other earring?" she asked as she turned.

Still not breathing, Ira looked up. She was built. He looked way up. Gawked.

She was Tess.

It was a Tess he'd never seen. A female Tess.

"You said you'd help me find my earring." She shook her head. "At this rate, we'll never make it out of this room."

He froze as she slid across the bed, thrusting her hand under a pillow. A glow of triumph lit up her face and she held up the other earring. She sat up again, leaning against him as she fastened it. "I thought that you were going to make the bed this time."

This time? "How long have we been here?"

"Two hours. Really, we'd better get downstairs. I don't know about you, but I'm starving."

It was eleven years in the future, and he was fooling around with Tess Norville at their tenth high school reunion. He caught sight of her left hand. The diamond on her engagement ring sparkled at him. A wedding band was above that.

Married. He couldn't believe it. Tess had never seemed that kind of girl.

He didn't like the idea that he had become the kind of guy who bounced into bed with a married woman. If it was his turn to make the bed *this time*, it stood to reason that they'd been having a great time doing what they weren't supposed to be doing at all.

"Your left cuff link is loose," Tess said. She was putting up her hair before the mirror. "Here, let me take care of it."

He held up his hand, then stared at it as she fastened the cuff link. He wore a gold wedding band. "Uh-h-h-h."

"There," she said, backing away. "This time it should stay." She turned before him. "How do I look?"

"Great." Underneath those khaki shirts, she had been hiding breasts. She was married. And fooling around.

He was married. And fooling around. This was depressing as hell, particularly since he had no memory of fooling around.

"It was sweet of you to phone Carl," Tess said. "I didn't realize that you knew his favorite book by heart." She began to recite softly. "'In an old house in Paris that was covered with vines . . .'"

As she moved aside from the night table, he saw a small framed photograph of two little boys, one near school age, the other an ankle-biter. Ira gaped. The older boy had red hair and a prominent nose.

Tess had red hair. Ira had a big nose. As the truth hit him, he started laughing.

"You're going to have to tell me what's so funny," she said.

"I just realized that we're married to each other." So this was what the computer had done to him! Had he mentioned Tess to the interviewer? He couldn't remember. The other possibility occurred to him. Maybe Tess had talked about him. Maybe she was the girl who'd told Barbara that she thought he was cute.

Here, in their hotel room, in her newly zipped form-fitting purple dress, she was certainly acting like she thought he was cute. Like she couldn't get enough of him. She turned back to the mirror and began applying lipstick. "Let me guess. Your mind was back in high school, when no one was married."

"Something like that." He got up and began straightening the bed, then glanced back at her. Tess looked good. Besides, this wasn't really happening. Anything could happen if nothing was really happening. *Anything*. "We don't really have to go downstairs right now, do we?" Maybe he wasn't using the right tone. He sounded more like he was pleading for a snack before dinnertime than trying to, well . . .

Tess's laugh was knowing even though he didn't know

what she knew. Ira tingled all over. "If we don't leave now, the party is likely to be over before we arrive. There are some people I want to see. I want—okay, I want them to know how well I've done. I want them to look at me. At us. At the boys." She picked up the photograph. "Who would have thought?"

Not him. That was for sure. He was married to Tess. She really liked him. He was a good father. "Hey, Tess?" he said casually. "When did you start liking me?"

"You know the answer to that."

"Tell me again." He went up behind her, wondering if he dared touch her. Wondering where he should touch her.

She bent her head to one side. "Junior high. Don't start looking smug again."

That long! The words came jumping out. "In junior high I thought you were a pain in the butt."

"In junior high . . ." She spoke softly. "I *was* a pain in the butt." She turned again. "Don't mess up my lipstick."

With a premonition that bordered on certainty, Ira became positive that he was going to mess up her lipstick.

He moved closer, then stopped. Something was wrong. She was taller than she should be.

Heels. She was wearing heels. And perfume.

He inhaled her.

"Ira," she said softly.

"Mm?" He kissed her and no bells rang.

"Good grief, Ira!" Tess laughed as they moved apart slightly. "That reminded me of our first kiss. You told me afterward that you had never kissed a girl."

"I told you that?" He couldn't have admitted that to her. He wouldn't.

"Not that you had to."

He glanced again at the picture of the two boys. "I'll tell you what. We'll keep trying until we get it right."

Both of them kept breaking up into laughter, which was good because it meant they were friends. Finally they connected and it was great. "Why did it take me so long?" he whispered into her hair. "Why do we fight every time we see each other?"

"You mean, why *did* we?" Her voice became sad. "I think we both knew that if anything happened, it would be serious."

"Scary stuff."

"Scary." She grabbed a tissue from the counter and gently wiped off the lipstick that had been transferred onto his face. She gave him a final quick kiss. "Go on, take care of your tie. I'll just be in the bathroom for a minute."

He watched her go. She even moved like a woman. He was humming as he faced himself in the mirror. Saw himself for the first time. Stared.

Ohgodohgodohgod.

"I'm bald," Ira whispered. His voice became louder. "*I have no hair.*"

"I'll be right out!" Tess called from the bathroom.

Feverishly he leaned closer to the mirror. Okay, he wasn't completely bald. He had a very high forehead that seemed to be spreading.

This time the computer had gone too far. Tess was good. The boys were good. Was hair some kind of trade-off?

He had to remember that this wasn't really happening.

Tess came out of the bathroom. "Downstairs," she said, putting the photo into her purse. "Now."

He held back. "Can I ask you a question?"

"Since when do you need permission?"

He was her husband. Husbands were allowed to ask their wives questions. Sixteen-year-olds still had to find their way.

He started. "Back when we were in school, you wore those big khaki jackets all the time."

While he was still trying to figure out how to word his question, she answered it for him. "I developed early. I put on camouflage gear because I hated the comments and I hated being grabbed."

"Except by me?" His voice couldn't have cracked. That kind of thing didn't happen to men.

She leaned forward, then seemed to remember her lipstick. "You never grabbed and you never stared. That's one of the things I always loved about you."

Ira made mental notes to himself. Back in his own time, he must never grab and he must never stare. "I don't get to stare?" he asked. "Not at all?"

"You noticed," she said, "after a while."

Noticing was in. Staring was out.

"Of course," Tess went on, "back in high school, the only girl you noticed was Sandra Wilcox."

Sandra! He hadn't thought of her once. He took in the room. No wonder the others were having so much trouble finding out simple details. This whole future thing was too complex, too involving. "Do you remember when Sandra died?" he asked.

"I remember how you went crazy for a while," she said softly. "I prepared that series for the school paper on teen suicides. I think it did some good. A few students went to talk with the counselor."

"It was a long time ago." Ira's heart began to thud again. More familiar. "How did she die? I mean, it was suicide, but how did she do it?"

Tess's reply seemed mechanical. "She stopped living."

"But how? Pills?"

"Nothing like that. She just . . . stopped."

The Tess he knew was exact about stating facts. "Did anyone know why she wanted to kill herself?" he persisted.

"I don't know that she wanted to." Her familiar smile had returned. "Come on, let's go find the others."

At least elevators hadn't changed. He was holding her hand as they emerged into the lobby. Just beyond was the crowded ballroom. Ira came to a dead halt in the doorway, dragging Tess back with him. It seemed so real—the plants, the glittering chandeliers, people holding drinks and laughing, the band in the background.

"You're trembling," she said.

In the elevator down he had been marveling at the way her hand felt like it belonged in his. Now he was clutching at her as though she were a life preserver. Abruptly he released her. "Sorry. I must be more nervous than I thought."

"It's your hair, isn't it?"

That was part of it. A draft was hitting the top of his

head. Never in his life had wind hit the top of his head without something running interference. "What hair?"

Her expression became serious. "Ira, do you see anyone in here who hasn't changed? At least this isn't like high school, where your entire day was ruined if you had a pimple. One advantage of being an adult is that we've been through more, so we have more self-confidence. Or at least, that's the way it's supposed to work." She paused. "If I was exactly the same as I was in high school, I'd be wearing a big khaki jacket."

"You ought to wear that again sometime," he said. Although this new, improved Tess seemed as much a miracle as their ultra-clear skin, in some ways he missed the old Tess. He and the real Tess exchanged mild insults. She kept him on his toes.

His "wife" squeezed his hand. "If anyone teases you, send them to me. I'll tell them that the rumor about bald men is true."

"What rumor?"

She gestured for him to lean over, then whispered into his ear. Whoa! "Now, let's go," she said. "I want to sample that fruit punch."

As they joined the crowd, Ira could see that Tess wasn't the only one who was thirsty. Graham was sitting at the bar, talking to Mac. Seedy, that's how Graham looked. He had spilled something on his shirt, and his tie would have been crappy even if the width was correct for that year. A thin, worried-looking woman stood next to him.

Ira shuddered when he thought of the real Graham. No wonder he had a fit.

Mac came over. "Hey, man." He clapped Ira's shoulder, and Ira pretended to sink.

He wasn't sure that he cared for the way Mac was looking Tess up and down. "Marriage agrees with you," the big man said to her finally. "I'm impressed."

"I understand that you're still on the loose," Tess said.

"So many women, so little time." Mac looked around. "Can I buy you two a drink?"

"A cola would be great," Ira answered. He glanced over at Graham. "He doesn't look so good."

"Yeah, well, I don't think I'd want to face his wife sober, either." The woman seemed to be trying to talk to Graham while he kept pulling away.

"I think I'll go and say hello to them." Tess moved away. "See you later."

"Later." Sweetheart. He almost called her sweetheart.

A waitress came over. Mac had his eye on her, that was for sure. He ordered Ira's cola and a beer for himself. "Mac," Ira started, "do you remember Sandra Wilcox?"

"Sure. Blonde. Sweet body." Mac shook his head. "Nobody figured that she'd do something like that. Heck of a waste."

"How did she kill herself?"

That same blank expression. "She stopped living."

"But how?"

Mac shook his head. "Search me. I just know it happened."

Some people were arguing nearby. Two women, judging from their voices. Ira looked around, but he couldn't figure out where the voices were coming from.

One woman had a heavy accent. *"So the boy is upset. The boy can consider this a warning."*

The other woman sounded something like Ms. Ruddley. Was she here? Ira couldn't spot her.

"This boy," she said levelly, *"did not need a warning. Life has already been his warning. He wanted something of value from this program."*

"The program shows what might be. In your studies, did you never see what happens when you take a mama alcoholic and a papa alcoholic? All of our research shows that this is the primary source of baby alcoholics. Nature and nurture."

"Not this boy!" Ms. Ruddley—he was positive now that it was her voice—spoke more loudly.

"Keep your voice down," the German woman ordered. *"He may be able to hear you."*

A pause. *"Do you mean that there's someone in there? Now?"*

Abruptly the argument ceased.

Mac spoke up again. "Do you remember that guy Sandra went out with in high school?"

"Patrick."

"I think that's him over there.'

Ira looked toward the corner of the room. The man he saw was approximately thirty. Definitely had all his hair. Was definitely Patrick. "Patrick wasn't in our class. What's he doing here?"

Mac's next words stunned him. "He married her best friend."

"Leanne." An unpleasant picture was forming.

"You have one great memory."

"Yeah." Ira started to walk away. "I'll catch up with you later."

"Too bad about your hair," Mac bawled after him.

Others turned to stare as he headed toward Patrick. Crap, it was Ira's hair and his head. Now that he had a chance to get used to the idea, he thought he didn't look so bad.

Tess was sitting at a table with Graham and his wife. The couple seemed to be relaxing with her, laughing and talking. She caught his eye and gestured for him to come over. He held up a hand indicating that he'd be there, soon. It was like they had their own private language.

He had to remember that this was not really happening. Argus only showed what might be. Sandra was in that category, but he had to know what happened.

"Patrick . . ."

Patrick turned. Ira had almost started thinking of himself as a man. This man reminded him once more that he was a boy taking part in an educational program.

Damn it, Patrick and Sandra had looked good together. He had a feeling that in another eleven years, they would have made a spectacularly handsome couple. The older Patrick was waiting for him to say something. "Sorry, I don't remember your name."

"Ira." Ira swallowed. "Ira Martinic. You're Patrick."

"You were a friend of Leanne's, right?"

Ira shook his head. "I knew Sandra."

A wave of pain passed through Patrick's eyes. When he spoke, his voice was husky. "That was a long time ago."

"I—I'm sorry." He needed to ask. "Look, my wife and I were talking. She was editor of the school paper. After it happened, Tess wrote a series on teen suicides. Only neither of us can remember what happened. I mean, it's been eleven years, right? So what happened?"

"She stopped living."

A slim brunette came up to Patrick and slipped her arm through his. This was Leanne. Sandra's former best friend.

"This is Ira," Patrick said to her. "He knew Sandy."

"Ira! For heaven's sake, I almost didn't recognize you."

He had no way of knowing how much time he had left. "I was wondering about Sandra," he said. "Whether you knew what happened."

"Not really." Leanne looked uncomfortable.

"You were her best friend," Ira persisted. "Girls are supposed to talk to each other about emotions and things." This wasn't getting him anywhere. "How did she die?"

Both of them had that flat expression. They almost chanted the words together. "She stopped—"

"Yes," he interrupted, "but how?" They looked at each other and then back at him. Ira was beginning to feel very strange about this. "What was the cause of death?"

"Her heart stopped." Patrick looked questioningly at his wife.

She nodded. "Her breathing stopped, too. That may have come first."

"Hey," Patrick said loudly. "This is a party, all right?"

THE NIGHT ROOM

Ira felt that he was being dismissed. He was the only sane person in this universe. He looked for another person he was positive was sane. Barbara.

He spotted her sitting near a far window and headed in her direction. She had reported that she was pregnant, but it was still a jolt to see her that way. "Hey, Barbara."

"Ira!" She began to stand, then laughed and stayed where she was. "Look at me. I'm as big as a house."

"An igloo," Ira said charitably as he pulled up a chair next to her. Chances were that he and Barbara had kept in contact through the years. "I'm glad that you could make it."

"I wouldn't have missed this for the world." They chatted for a few minutes, and Barbara pointed out Joy. "Who else have you talked to?" she asked.

"Patrick." This was his chance. "He used to go with Sandra Wilcox."

"You liked her. Only you never said anything." She looked thoughtful. "You were so broken up, walking around the school in a daze. I remember when Tess started yelling at you to get your act together. I really thought that she'd blown it, like nothing would ever happen between you." Abruptly Barbara sat up straight. "Ouch, that was a good one. This baby is quite a kicker. Tess says that your two were lively."

"About Sandra," he persisted. "Do you remember how she died?"

Please don't say that she stopped living.

"It was so sad. Sandra stopped living."

And Barbara, who couldn't even keep her crayons inside

the lines of a coloring book, designed clothes. This had gone far enough. The band was just concluding a number when Ira strode up to the platform. The microphone squawked in his hand. "Hey!" he called as faces turned toward him. "Listen up! I have a question here." A buzz of conversation went around the room. "I've been trying to find out what happened to Sandra Wilcox. It's important. I know this was a long time ago, but I need to know. I was in love with her, okay? Or maybe I thought I was. I'm married now. It looks like everything is great, but I still want to know what happened to Sandra Wilcox. How did she kill herself? Why? Did her boyfriend leave her for her best friend?"

"*Ira!*" At the table, Tess was standing up.

Someone was moving toward him. Patrick. He jumped up on the platform, a murderous look in his eye. Something very large and very hard slammed into Ira's jaw. The chandelier swam before his eyes, followed by the piano. Followed by the floor.

"Time to wake up," Karen said. "Did you have a nice dream?"

* * *

* *

15 *

"This whole thing is totally ridiculous," Tess said. While Ira was in the Night Room, Barbara had filled her in on the Sandra situation.

The four had decided to wait for Ms. Ruddley to finish speaking with Graham. Twenty minutes had passed since Ira's return. In that time, he had been sneaking peeks at Tess's face. She was uptight. She was impatient.

This was not the woman he married.

They all looked up when Karen came into the waiting room wearing a purple ski jacket. She was pulling on wool gloves. "You're all still here."

Barbara stood and stretched. "Will Ms. Ruddley be out soon?"

The assistant stood there. "She left a while ago. She was going to take that boy home, the one who was so upset."

"Maybe we can call her at home," Ira said. The others headed toward the coatrack, muttering their discontent.

"I don't think she'll be there." Karen looked uneasy. "She made a phone call from my office, something about an illness in her family. I gathered that she was going to drop off the boy at his home, then drive straight to the airport."

"The *boy's* name is Graham," Tess said.

"Graham's coat is still here." Ira took down a green parka with frayed cuffs. "I can bring it to him at school."

"Karen," Barbara said as she zipped her jacket, "we were wondering about something. The interviews are supposed to eliminate anyone who is severely depressed. What would happen if a person with suicidal tendencies got through?"

The assistant was obviously used to student questions. "Eleven years down the road, their life situations will have changed. That's all I can say with certainty."

"This is what we want to know." Tess spoke levelly. "If someone seems likely to commit suicide now, is it possible that the program will show that she died?"

"I think you're forgetting that Argus's information comes from interviewers and questionnaires," Karen said. "Anyone with suicidal tendencies would be channeled toward counseling." She paused. "I can't see any value that Argus would have for someone without a future, can you?" She herded them toward the door.

"How about, like, for a warning?" Mac suggested when they reached the hallway. "Like, if you kill yourself, you're going to miss a great party."

"Argus shows what might lie ahead so people can make decisions. Once you die, you're all out of decisions. Guys," Karen said, "this is a really interesting topic, but I want to go home now." She held open one of the outside doors. "My suggestion is that you all go out for coffee together and talk until you wind down."

"Wait," Ira protested when they reached the steps. "When is Sandra's appointment?"

"Who?" Karen was locking the door behind her.

"The one who had to be postponed," Tess said.

"Number seven—six, I mean." Karen walked away across the parking lot. "She's been rescheduled for Monday afternoon."

Nobody seemed to know what to say. Mac took out his keys but made no move toward the cars. "This is nuts."

Everything about this night was nuts.

"Ira, my folks can give you a ride home," Barbara offered. He still felt light-headed from the Night Room, so he'd already decided to pick up his car the next morning.

"He's on my way," Tess said gruffly. "I can take him."

"Thanks," Ira said to her. "I didn't know you cared."

"Huh." She dug out her own keys. "If you were involved in an accident, you'd probably ruin somebody's Christmas."

Barbara moved down the stairs. "My mom is waiting for me in her office. I guess I'll see you all tomorrow at school."

"Wait," Ira said. "Maybe it's a good idea to go for coffee. To talk. I mean, what happens if we can't reach Ms. Ruddley? We have to tell somebody."

"Sandra," Tess said. "You should tell Sandra."

"Not Sandra." Barbara looked startled. "She's the last person you should tell."

"But if Argus says that she's going to commit—"

"She might do it just because Argus says it's going to happen. Some people are like that."

Some people might find themselves attracted to a girl because Argus said it was meant to be. "I agree," Ira said. "Besides, if we told her, then we'd have to tell her everything. *Everything*." *Everything* included seeing Leanne and Patrick in the future, married.

"Jeez," Mac said, speaking for all of them.

While Barbara went to tell her mother that Tess would bring her home later, they talked over which cars to take. Mac swore that he was all right, but Tess was the only one absolutely unaffected by events in the Night Room. They were half-frozen by the time they all piled into her ancient VW and headed toward the nearest shopping area. Mac sat in front, complaining about the tight fit.

"So, what do you feel like eating?" As they left the university grounds, Tess drove slowly down residential streets twinkling with Christmas lights. "Burgers, Chinese food . . . ?"

"I want something bland," Barbara answered. "A turkey sandwich sounds good."

"I forgot," Mac said. "The little mother is eating for two. No Szechuan Chinese. Okay, I want someplace where I can get a couple of burgers. Fries. A thick malt." He grinned. "Hey, I think my appetite is coming back."

Recovery time seemed to have something to do with how much you'd changed. From what Mac said, eleven years hadn't altered him much. "I'm not very hungry," Ira said, "but I'll order something. Otherwise they're likely to find me hanging up in a field somewhere scaring the birds."

Tess must have had other things on her mind. She spared him the obvious response. "How about Denny's?" she suggested.

"Anyplace," Barbara said tiredly. "As long as it's warm and we can all sit together."

"We'll need privacy," Ira said. They wouldn't want their conversation overheard.

"How about the House of Pancakes?" Barbara suggested.

"There's the A&W," Mac said, pointing off to his right. "Oh, right, no turkey sandwiches for—"

"Don't say it again," Barbara warned him.

They had just pulled up to a light when Ira spotted a familiar-looking blue car parked across the street in front of a jewelry store. "That's Patrick's car," he said. "I recognize the bumper sticker." HE'S DEAD, JIM. YOU GRAB HIS TRICORDER.

The door of the jewelry store opened. Patrick came out with a laughing girl who wasn't Sandra. "That's Leanne," Tess said. She pulled forward.

"What are you doing?" Ira demanded.

"The light changed," Tess said. "I'll circle back." They returned to the same area in time to watch Patrick holding the girl's arm while he helped her in.

"She's not bad-looking," Mac said as Patrick got in. "I almost forgot which girl she was. Leanne, huh?"

Patrick's sedan pulled out.

"Follow that car," Ira said.

*

*

*

*

*

16

*

"I *may* drive behind that car for a while," Tess stated. "I refuse to *follow* that car. This is night. Some side streets are icy."

"Yeah, yeah, yeah," Mac muttered.

Ira craned his neck, trying to see what was going on in the car in front of them. The two inside certainly acted like a couple. They seemed pleased with themselves.

"Let me drive," Mac said.

"My car?" Tess yelped. "Not on your life. Not even if you hadn't just come out of the Night Room. Not ever."

"She's right," Ira said. "We've seen enough."

They hadn't. Just then, fate intervened. Patrick's car turned into the parking lot of the White Spot. "Huh." Mac laughed. "It looks like we're not the only ones having a snack attack."

"Let me guess," Tess said. "Everybody wants to go to the White Spot."

She had to make another circle of the block to get back. As they walked into the warm restaurant, Ira spotted Patrick and Leanne sitting at a far table. They were scanning menus.

The restaurant was only a third full, so their group was ushered in immediately. The waitress seemed to be leading them to a table close to the entrance when Barbara stopped her. "Excuse me," she said, pointing at a booth that was near Patrick and Leanne. "Do you think we could sit there?"

Ira and Mac groaned. Booths were fine when you didn't have long legs.

"That's fine." The waitress handed out menus as the girls got in first. Ira slid in next to Tess.

As they scanned the menu, they kept glancing toward Patrick and Leanne.

The waitress came back with glasses of water. At the other table, Leanne was holding up her hand to admire a ring. Patrick sat back looking pleased.

Barbara and Ira ordered turkey sandwiches while Mac had two burgers with fries. Tess settled for hot chocolate. "I wonder if this makes me an investigative reporter," she mused as she watched her marshmallows melt. "I wonder when you stop feeling like some kind of Peeping Tom."

"You're not going to put this in the paper," Ira said.

She looked up at him impatiently. "I'm not planning to endanger anyone's life, if that's what you mean. But after all this is over, you can bet that I'm going to write about Argus. Just look at what it's done to everybody."

Graham had freaked. Joy had been crying. Barbara hadn't said much beyond wondering why Argus had seen her as a fashion designer. Ira had found the experience unsettling in one way and reassuring in another.

Only Mac seemed unaffected as he bit ravenously into his first burger. Snap! Snap! and it was gone. Ira felt like he was watching feeding time at the zoo. "Hey," Mac said when he looked up. "I'm in training, okay?"

Tess sipped her chocolate. Abruptly she put down her cup. "They've spotted us," she said in a low voice.

Ira turned slightly. Patrick was saying something to Leanne. She turned toward them.

"Wave." Tess matched her action to her word.

They all waved. "This is ridiculous," Ira mumbled. "I know her—not well, though."

The couple seemed worried. As Patrick went over to the cash register to pay, Leanne came to their booth. "Hi."

They murmured their greetings.

"How're you doing?" Mac asked.

"Okay." The brunette girl stood there. "Wasn't your class supposed to go through the Argus project tonight?"

"We're finished," Ira answered. "Sandra Wilcox is a friend of yours, right?"

She nodded. Patrick had come up next to her.

"They didn't have time for everybody tonight," Tess explained. "Sandra was sent home."

The two exchanged uneasy looks. "What time did she leave?" Patrick asked.

"Six-thirty or so," Barbara answered. "We weren't sup posed to eat beforehand, so we're all starving."

Patrick muttered something that sounded like a swear word. He and Leanne went off a short distance to consult. Leanne came back to the booth. "Um, look," she said. "We'd appreciate it if you didn't mention seeing us together tonight."

Ira stiffened.

"That's your business," Mac said. He gave her a slow smile. "That's a nice sweater."

"Thanks." She seemed flustered. "Well, I'll see you."

The two left. "Leanne's not bad," Mac said as he picked up his burger and took a big bite.

"That depends on your definition of *bad*," Tess said.

"Hey," Mac protested. "A lot of people believe that girls and guys can just be friends. I'm not one of them, but that might be what's going on here."

"It's true." Barbara looked jarred at hearing such wisdom from Mac. "Ira and I have been pals for years. Nothing romantic is ever going to happen, and we both know it."

He had harbored romantic thoughts toward Barbara now and then, but in a general way reserved for all girls he liked or admired. "So maybe Leanne wasn't doing anything tonight, and Patrick wanted a break from studying. They both figured that Sandra was going to be busy."

"Then why would they ask us to keep it a secret?" Tess grated out. "Darn. I wouldn't have mentioned seeing them, but now I've become a conspirator."

She seemed genuinely upset. "Hey," Ira said. "It's okay."

Tess blinked as she shook her head.

Mac stretched his legs. "Did you see the way she was looking at me?" A pause.

"Who?" Ira asked for all of them.

"Leanne, of course."

"No," Ira said flatly. "Tell us how she was looking at you."

"She was nervous," Barbara said.

"There were signals," Mac said. "Invisible signals."

Obviously his favorite kind.

He looked at their faces, one by one. "I thought you guys were all so smart. I have this whole thing figured out."

"It's been a rough night," Ira said. "Tell us."

"Okay." Mac lowered his voice and leaned forward, which had the effect of making the others lean forward at the same time. "You're saying that Sandra kills herself because Leanne has been moving in on Patrick. Suppose that I move in on Leanne—for a while, I mean."

Three pairs of eyes widened.

17

Graham stood in the street until the counselor drove away. Ms. Ruddley would be back at school sometime next week, she said. They'd talk more.

He swore. The whole thing had been bull. The college still had his jacket, too. He took a last deep breath of cold night air before he let himself into the apartment building with its odor of old cooking smells. The elevator didn't respond to the button, but that was okay. He needed to move, and four flights of stairs weren't about to kill him.

Man. Man, this had not turned out like he expected.

"Graham?" his mother called when he let himself in. "Graham, is that you?"

"It's me." He went over to the couch. His mother was lying where he'd left her that morning.

"What time is it?"

He told her. She sat up slowly. "I must've fallen asleep. I forget—where did you go?"

"Something for school," he mumbled.

"Oh, sure. They were paying you, right?"

He shook his head.

"No point to it, then."

"No point," he echoed. He stared out the window toward a neon sign that flashed on and off all night. "Anyway, they messed up. Maybe I'll get another turn."

She headed toward the bathroom. "They should pay you."

They owed him a *real* turn. That was for sure.

At home, Tess found her father sitting alone in the living room. "How did it go tonight?" he asked.

"Okay."

"Did you see the future?"

"No one can see the future."

"I wish I could have when I was your age." He marked the page in his book and closed it. "I wish to hell that I could have known what was coming."

Tess looked around. "Where's Petey?"

"In bed. Your mother went out to a movie with Sheila— some kind of shoot-'em-up."

Sheila was her mother's closest friend. "Why didn't you go, too?"

He lifted one shoulder. "I have work to do."

"Did you and Petey do anything?"

"He watched some TV." He sighed. "In another two years, you'll be leaving for college."

"Petey will still be here. And Mom. That's the future." No answer. "I'm not charging for the prediction."

"I wouldn't pay you," her father said.

As he let himself into the apartment, Mac saw a red scarf hung over one of the table lamps, which was supposed to give the place a romantic effect. At least, that was what his dad always said. It was also a warning: WOMAN PRESENT.

He could see through to the hall. His father's bedroom door was closed. Probably he'd gotten lucky.

A low murmur of voices came from the room, plus a woman's light laugh. Yep.

Mac almost tripped over a high-heeled black shoe near the couch. Two wineglasses were on the coffee table, one with a final inch of wine. He sat down and drained it, then looked around at the supper dishes still on the table.

Some of his dad's ladies liked to clean. Either this one didn't, or they'd been in a hurry. One side of him hated a mess. The other side hated to clean up somebody else's mess.

He straightened up the place a little, and after that he brushed his teeth. He smiled at himself in the mirror. He had great teeth. That was one of the first things he'd checked out when he hit the reunion party.

Too bad he couldn't have stuck around to see how things came out with the waitress. Maybe he could meet her again sometime when the new improved version of Argus came out.

Ira stared at the ceiling of his room and thought about Tess. And Carl. And Bob.

And Sandra.

He punched his pillow in frustration. Why did Tess have to be so darned prickly? In a lot of ways, he wanted to take another turn at Argus so he could see her again, find out what else had changed during those eleven years.

When Barbara reached the privacy of her own room, she took out a pad of paper. She began to sketch the figure of a woman, just to see if she had missed noticing that she was artistic. Finally she laid the drawing aside.

She had no talent for art at all. She felt curiously unaffected by the man who was supposed to be her husband. Carlo. Oh, perhaps she was, a little. He'd been both handsome and nice. The possibility of that combination had never occurred to her. If nothing else, she had discovered a prejudice of which she had been unaware.

She pressed her hands against her flat belly. When she had told her parents about discovering her advanced pregnancy, their first reaction was to laugh. Okay, it was funny.

In bed, she lay on her stomach. It was flat. Nothing was there. Nothing. As she dropped off to sleep, her last thought was that she wouldn't mind having a look at Melanie.

———

"Sandra? Is it too late to call?"

By her clock radio, it was almost eleven. She had a private phone line in her bedroom, and she'd been lying there reading. Now, as whenever she heard his voice, a thrill ran through her. "Hi, Patrick," she answered softly. "I called your dorm earlier. You weren't there. Too bad. They let me go early."

He cleared his throat. "I went driving around for a while. Hey, I missed you."

"I missed you, too," Sandra said. "It's too bad. We could have gone out together and looked at the lights."

They made a date for the next night to drive around and look at the Christmas lights, then talked for a few minutes more. After she hung up, she picked up his framed picture and hugged it to her chest. No matter what Argus said, she was positive that Patrick would be in her future.

Life without him was unthinkable.

18

Dr. Halstrom sat alone at a table in the staff lounge, which was illuminated solely by the soft glow from dispensing machines. She had just finished another cup of the thick black coffee she preferred—coffee she could sink her teeth into. She never minded drinking what was left in the bottom of the pot at the end of the day. If that was gone, she would chew the pot itself.

She stubbed out her cigarette in the metal ashtray she had brought from her office. By university edict, no smoking was allowed in the buildings. Alone after hours, that was something else. The air-conditioning system would cleanse her sins.

Perhaps she was so weary tonight because she had been dealing with high school children.

The girl was intelligent. The girl had her reasons for not wishing to take part, and Dr. Halstrom had not listened. Perhaps she should have. The girl would become a journalist, and she could be useful.

No, the girl was a child.

Her headache had intensified. She had already swallowed the two pain pills that the doctor allowed her each day. She would take another when she arrived home, in order that she might sleep. The doctors did not know everything, just as the school counselor did not understand about the boy who wanted to work with his hands. Number four.

"This boy did not need a warning. He wanted something of value from this program."

She had given him something of great value.

She had known boys who came from families such as his. Time would pass, he would grow older, and he would work side by side with others. Dust would accumulate in his throat, the dust of honest labor. Someone would say it: "*Let us go to the tavern. Let us wash the dust away.*" Sooner or later the reasoning would come: "*I am not my father, who was weak and who could not drink. I am not my mother.*"

She had allowed the boy to see himself as weak. He would never forgive her, of course, as long as he lived. That was fine. She was not after love.

Her vision was beginning to blur. She rubbed her eyes to clear them, then reached down for her cane. Time to go to her tiny apartment near the campus.

She returned to her office and put the ashtray into a drawer. Through the one-way glass window she could see into the Night Room. *Like a morgue.* This joke had come from a newly hired assistant, on his first day. To the stark astonishment of the highly qualified young man, she dismissed him on the spot. Karen respected Argus. This was all she required.

The low lights were on, the same as they had been when the last boy had left. Number Five, the one with the prominent nose. A girl had been rescheduled to Monday. It was a good night's work.

Rolfe would be proud of her.

Rolfe had always been proud of her.

She picked up the framed photograph on her desk. It showed two skiers smiling at the camera, the man in red and the woman in blue. His arm was around her waist, while behind them the sun beat down on a field of snow.

They had truly believed that life would go on like that forever. Rolfe had loved her, simply and well, with open hands and heart.

Dr. Halstrom blinked. "I am not that woman."

But of course you are, my darling.

"I've changed," she said. "I'm older."

Bosh!

She thought of the disks in her locked bottom drawer, her own special programs. Her head continued to pound. "Not tonight," she said. "My head throbs. I would be poor company for you."

Inside her office, she dimmed the Night Room until it was completely black, and then she left. The only light that still shone came from the drawer in which Argus slept.

"Joy! Get up, you're going to be late for school." Her mother pushed open the bedroom door. "Come on, sleepy-head."

Joy lay in bed with the covers pulled high under her chin. "I don't feel very well."

"You were fine last night." Mrs. Abercrombie came into the room. She placed the back of her hand against her daughter's forehead. "No fever."

Joy moaned. "My stomach hurts."

"Did you eat anything when you got home?"

She hadn't felt very hungry, but she had eaten the small portions allowed by her diet. "Not much."

Her mother stood there for a minute. "I have my computer course this morning. Will you be all right on your own?"

"I think so," Joy said. "I'll watch TV or something."

"All right, then. I'll phone your school."

Joy turned over on her side as the door closed. She didn't feel sick. She couldn't face the others after the Night Room.

Ira woke up before his alarm could ring. He put both hands on his head.

He still had all his hair.

"Oh, my gosh, I know what happened!" Barbara was sitting at the breakfast table with her parents. "About the sportswear. I must have told the interviewer that I was interested in designer genes. G-E-N-E-S. She heard designer jeans, like denims."

"Chances are that a similar error occurred regarding Sandra," her father said. "I think you should tell her."

"Wait." Her mother put down the slice of toast she was nibbling. "I've been thinking about this. The people at the party are computer images and can only pass along information generated by Argus. Suicide might mean something different to a computer. Examine the word: -cide means killing, sui- means oneself. A terminal illness might qualify as suicide since the body kills itself—death due to an internal malfunction."

An illness hadn't occurred to Barbara. "Sandra looks healthy."

"Her heart?" Her father shook his head. "She wouldn't be allowed into the program at all. I'm particularly puzzled by the specific time frame."

"I'll find out when Ms. Ruddley is coming back," Barbara said. "It has to be some kind of stupid mistake. After all, Argus had me designing sportswear and married to Carlo." Who was undoubtedly a hunk.

"About your pregnancy," her mother said. "I understand this almost qualifies as a trend. I don't mean that each group finds itself with a pregnant student. Still, the number seems out of proportion to the general population. Another thing. These students tend to be extremely intelligent."

"A problem with the program?" Barbara asked.

"Possibly with the program's creator."

Barbara knew that the personality and beliefs of a programmer could easily invade her program. "Argus was still interesting. I'd like to try the improved version when it comes out."

Her parents exchanged glances.

"Everyone says that," her father replied mildly. "I've never heard of any student who didn't want to go back." He looked at his wife. "Do you think there's a posthypnotic command to return? Say, a subliminal sales pitch? Argus is nonprofit now, but it could easily find a commercial market."

"The explanation may be something more mundane," her mother said, "like the rush of adrenaline experienced at an amusement park. The experience is extremely stimulating. One wishes to return—eventually."

"I wonder what changes will be made," Barbara said.

"*Night Room, Part II,*" her father intoned as though it were a horror movie. "Bring on the popcorn."

There was one student who would never want to return. Barbara was sure of it.

Graham.

*   *
*
*   *
2   *

Ira was surprised to see Graham at school. "You're here," he blurted out when he spotted the thin boy walking through the main corridor before first period.

Graham was wearing a heavy plaid work shirt over a sweatshirt. "Is there some reason I shouldn't be?"

"No! I mean . . ." Ira wasn't sure what to say. The last time he'd seen Graham, he'd been practically puking his guts out on the campus lawn. "Tess took your parka. It's in her car."

"I'll connect with her later." Graham stood there. "Look," he said gruffly, "the computer was wrong, that's all. You saw how it was wrong about Barbara."

"Definitely."

"So it was wrong about me. Ms. Ruddley explained about how the program works. Like, it makes book on how we're all going to turn out." His laugh was ugly. "Nice program." His expression changed. "Hey, weren't you married to—oomph!"

Ira wasn't able to think of anything else to do, so he slammed his books into Graham's stomach. The other boy just stood there with a surprised look on his face.

"Sorry, man," Ira said, "but don't say it. Okay?"

He didn't know what he expected, but not the silent

laughter that shook the other boy's narrow frame. At last Graham stopped. He formed the name silently. Tess.

Ira shuddered in an exaggerated way. "Nobody else knows."

Graham's expression had lightened. "That makes the computer wrong at least three times. Barbara said it was absolutely wrong about her. As for you and—"

Ira gave him a warning look.

"You two don't get along at all. At the reunion, she didn't even act like herself. I can't remember much except that she was nice. You two were laughing and holding hands and everything, like a real couple."

Graham should have seen them in the hotel room Ira forced a laugh. "Not too likely, huh?"

"My mom said that they should pay people to go through Argus. She's right." He chuckled. "I wouldn't mind trying that design-your-own version when it comes out. Maybe by then they'll figure how to make it work." The buzzer sounded. "Look, I won't say anything about you and . . . you know. So maybe you don't have to tell anybody about me freaking out."

After first period Barbara called to Ira in the hall. She was with Tess.

"An illness?" Ira felt stunned when he heard Dr. Flores's theory. "You mean, like maybe there was something on her medical form. Something serious."

"Oh, come on," Tess protested. "Nobody signs up for Argus unless she expects to be around for her tenth reunion."

None of them said what they were thinking, that maybe Sandra didn't know. Maybe her parents were waiting to break the news to her. "It's possible," Barbara said.

Tess snorted. "And I'm really looking forward to seeing your latest swimsuit designs."

Ms. Ruddley wouldn't be back next week because of a family illness. Only a short time remained until Christmas vacation, so she might not return until January.

"I'll see if my parents have any other suggestions." Barbara thought. "Dr. Halstrom is away giving a lecture. What about Karen?"

"I already left a message for Karen to phone me at the *Banner* office. Frankly, though, I think everybody is taking this whole Argus thing too seriously—starting with its creator." Tess grimaced. "You should have seen Dr. Halstrom's face when I said I wanted out."

"She was ticked off?" Ira was surprised. After all, Ms. Ruddley had stressed that they could drop out at any time.

"Not exactly mad. Contemptuous. I think she pitied me. You heard Barbara—Argus is Dr. Halstrom's baby. No mother likes to see her baby ignored. She pushed a button on her keyboard, and I was out. '*You were number six. Now you are not.*'"

Just then, Sandra passed them in the hall. She was walking with Leanne, both of them deep in conversation.

"She looks very well," Barbara observed.

"She looks great," Ira said. It was the truth. She must have just come in from the cold, because her cheeks were glowing. The warning buzzer sounded. "I have to get to class. Let's see what happens with Plan A." Mac was Plan A.

"I could interview Sandra," Tess said suddenly. "After all, she's running for student council, and the election is just before the holiday break. Maybe I can see her this weekend. That way I can ask her opinion on all sorts of things."

"Teenage depression," Barbara itemized. "Counseling . . . the crisis hot line. You'll be making suggestions at the same time. Subtle, very subtle."

"It's a great idea." Ira also thought it would be a great idea if Tess would stop scowling at him every time he complimented her. "That's Plan B," he said. "Go for it."

Sandra and Leanne were standing in line for the drinking fountain. "How do you do it?" Leanne teased. "Did you see the way that boy was looking at you? The boy with the big nose, I mean."

"That's Ira. He's in one of my classes."

"If you ask me," Leanne said, "I think he thinks of you as more than a classmate."

"Maybe." She paused. "I phoned you last night when I got home. Where were you?"

The boy at the fountain was moving away. "I did a bit of Christmas shopping," Leanne answered as she took his place. She didn't meet Sandra's eyes.

"Alone?"

"Hardly. The stores were jammed." She straightened and looked at her watch. "Oops, I have to get to the library."

3

Did they think that asking out a girl was some kind of spectator sport? Mac couldn't believe that Tess and Ira both planned to watch him ambush Leanne in the hall before fifth period. As he moved toward her English classroom, the two followed behind him like kids on a field trip. "This is ridiculous," he sputtered when they stopped near the door.

"I have English with Leanne," Tess explained. "I belong here. If necessary, I can help you look respectable. Ira and I will be talking."

"I don't need your help." And he sure didn't need an audience. Just then, he spotted his quarry coming down the hall. He decided not to say anything until she was almost to the door. "Hey, Leanne."

She turned. "Oh, hi . . . Mac."

He had never in his life waited for any girl to show up. Only a few feet away, Ira was pretending to copy Tess's History notes. "So, how's it going?" he asked.

"Okay. I'm looking forward to the Christmas break."

He nodded. "Christmas. Right."

"I still have some more shopping to do. I have a big family."

"There's just my dad and me."

"But you get a tree at least, right?"

He shook his head. "Not since I was little." His mom was the one who used to see to that kind of thing.

"I guess everybody's different. Christmas is a big deal at our house."

Mac couldn't figure out how they'd gotten stuck talking about Christmas. He tried to think of the best move to make. Christmas, okay. He gave her his never-fail smile. "I bet you hang up mistletoe and everything. Maybe I should drop in and visit you."

Smooth, very smooth, he congratulated himself.

Her laughter startled him. "I've heard about you," she said.

"Yeah?" Now she was onto his favorite subject—Mac himself. "What did you hear?"

"Oh." Tess was looking in his direction. Ira nudged her, and she stopped. "You think you're somebody."

Mac didn't just *think* he was somebody. He decided to make an effort to sound humble. "Everybody is somebody." Then he grinned, which probably spoiled it. "So, who's talking about me?"

"Lots of girls."

"Sounds about right."

"Nobody's said anything really bad."

"Not even—" He caught himself in time. "Good," he said instead.

"Not even Sandra," she said, misunderstanding him. "She just wishes that you'd stop making embarrassing remarks."

"Okay," he said. "I'll stop making remarks. That'll be my New Year's whatdoyoucallit."

"Resolution." Of course, it wasn't New Year's yet.

He was running out of things to say. "So, are you seeing anybody or anything?" Sandra's boyfriend, for instance.

She seemed to need to think before she answered. "I'm not seeing anyone seriously," she replied at last.

"Okay," he said. "So maybe I'll give you a call sometime."

She had to think about that, too. Mac found to his surprise that he was actually starting to worry that she'd say no. "Okay."

"Okay?" His grin was real. "Great." He took a step back, almost colliding with the door. He gulped. "See you." He started to walk away but stopped when he saw Tess gesturing at him. She was making small circles in the air. Ira held something up to his ear and pretended to talk. Mac got it. He went back to Leanne. "Your phone number. I need your number."

"Good going." She was laughing at him again.

This girl didn't understand that he was supposed to be treated with respect. He opened his notebook. "Okay, shoot."

For a second, he wondered whether she'd changed her mind. Then she told him her number and walked into the classroom, leaving him standing there.

A few seconds later, Ira was at his left side and Tess at his right. "So, how did it go?" Ira demanded.

"How did it look like it went?" Mac asked casually.

"She didn't spit in his eye," Ira said to Tess.

"Nothing to it. Hey, what do you expect?" Mac shut his notebook. "So, maybe I'll give her a call in a week or so."

"Tonight," Tess said.

"This afternoon." Ira looked serious. "After school."

"Hey." He backed up. "No." He couldn't believe this "Are you both completely ignorant?" He had to consider who he was talking to. Tess. Ira. Both completely ignorant. "Let me tell you how these things work."

"Oh, good," Tess said. "This should be fascinating."

He decided to talk straight to Ira and let Tess listen in. "See, you meet a girl. And maybe you think she's—" He glanced uneasily at Tess.

"Interesting," Ira filled in for him. "A great conversation-alist."

"Whatever. The thing is that you don't want her to think you're interested."

"Why not?" Tess asked.

This was worse than he thought. "Because then she'll think, like, that she's got you."

Ira and Tess both looked puzzled.

Jeez. "Women are like that. Trust me."

"If you like a girl," Tess said, "and you call her right away, you mean that she'll think that you're her boyfriend . . . even though you've only just met." She shook her head. "Sorry, I don't understand."

"Maybe he means something like *Romeo and Juliet*," Ira suggested. "Love at first sight, unto death." Both looked back at Mac. "Is that it?"

"Wait!" Tess said. "I think I know. You're afraid that she'll get self-confident."

A self-confident woman was bad. "Yeah." That wasn't exactly it, but it was close. Uncertain women were more cooperative. If you showed a girl that you were interested, she could get you twisted all out of shape.

Ira's expression was dead serious. "This is an emergency."

"Aw, man." Mac groaned.

"Chicken." Tess clucked softly.

"I suppose that *I* could ask her out instead," Ira offered.

Maybe it was Mac's imagination, but Tess's frown seemed to darken. Mac shook his head. "You wouldn't have a prayer with a girl like that."

Now Tess seemed irritated at *him*. "How on earth can you know something like that?"

Like Leanne would go for a big-nosed geek. Sure.

It took a big man to do a big deed. Mac squared his shoulders. "I'll call her tonight."

Maybe it was his imagination, but as he walked away, he could swear that he heard the crowd roar its approval.

Ira turned to grin at Tess. So far, Plan A was a go.

She didn't favor him with a smile in return. "Read the article I gave you," she told him as she headed into the classroom. "It's relevant."

4

The article was from a speech at a science fiction convention held several years earlier: THE HOLODECK AS OPIUM DEN. Ira dug it out in study hall and began to read.

> Sometimes this writer worries about the crew of the mighty starship Enterprise. They have at their disposal one of the most mind-blowing inventions ever—the holodeck—and, with almost no exceptions, what do they use it for? Recreation and education.
>
> These activities are sane and as wholesome as oatmeal. But how about working off frustration by, say, blasting the captain into atomic particles? If the holodeck were ever truly utilized, a new definition of mental illness would be needed. You can do what you want in the holodeck. Try the same thing outside, and you're one sick puppy.

Ira skimmed down a few paragraphs.

> And what of the holo-deprived? Hey, folks, when I was young, my family was so poor that I had to play with real children. The first girl I kissed looked like an ordinary person. And, oh yeah, I had to get to know her first.
>
> Does anyone remember a time before VCRs?

Let's see a show of hands. Fewer each year. Let me explain how things worked in the olden days. When you wanted to watch a scheduled program, you had to be at home in front of the television. Your great-grandparents used to gather before the radio.

I'm going to apply the VCR analogy to marriage. I assume that most of you know that a marriage will not last if you treat your spouse as you would a taped program. Click—now I am in the mood to be married. Click—now I'm not. Never mind skimming the channels. Our ideal is one partner forever, as in-separable as Desi and Lucy.

Yes, I know. But not in reruns.

Interesting, Ira supposed. But he still didn't see what this had to do with Argus.

Dating? [Cringe.] Why bother?

Now he was getting interested.

Or, for courtship junkies, why do anything else?

Marriage. Let us say that I have my career, which is satisfying but demanding. I have friends. I want to be married as long as my convenience is served and nothing is asked of me. I believe that I can handle marriage for one hour a day. Maybe not every day, however. Maybe not the same hour.

Sound good? Try the holodeck.

Let us talk about real love in real life. Sometimes people stop loving us. Sometimes we stop loving them first and they hang around our necks like a rotting albatross. The holodeck solution: repro-gram. What is a healthy relationship in the day of the holodeck? Do we stay together for the sake of the children, if the children are also on software? Do we love them less?

An opiate? You bet. What is more addictive than love?

He finished the article. Then he thought about Tess, not the real Tess but the one he had met in the hotel room. He wondered just how real she was.

5

"Hey, Leanne." Mac had to dial three times before he got her number right. "Are you busy tomorrow night?"

"Tomorrow?" She paused. "Saturday?"

He had dishes soaking in the sink. He was doing the laundry, too. The laundry-room schedule gave their apartment one afternoon each week and one evening. "Saturday, right. I thought, a movie." He waited for her to say that she already had plans.

She didn't. "I have to be home by eleven."

"Saturday," Mac stressed. He waited. "Let me guess. During the week, you have to be in by nine."

"Nine-thirty, actually. Except that I'm really not supposed to date at all during the week."

Uh-huh. Mac didn't have a newspaper. "See if you can find something that starts around seven-thirty, okay?"

"There's probably a Disney film playing somewhere. We can take my little sister. She's eight." She paused. "Mac? Are you still there?"

Was this some kind of a test? "That's cool." He was beginning to enjoy himself. "I get along okay with kids."

"I think she's probably seen every suitable film," Leanne said at last. She fetched the newspaper listings, and then they discussed films. Both liked westerns. A new one was playing.

Not so bad, he congratulated himself as he hung up. The stove timer went off. He was whistling as he went downstairs to change the laundry over to the dryer.

6

Why wasn't there any coverage?

Michael had been watching the TV and listening to the radio since Thursday evening. The local stations should have been screaming the story, followed by the national ones. The paper, ditto. By now it should be front-page news.

He was cruising the channels as his mother came into the living room. Somebody had won a lottery. Crime on our streets . . . blah, blah. He muted the TV and turned toward her. "Suppose," he said, "suppose you knew that something had happened, something that should be on the news. Suppose it wasn't."

"Are you expecting to see something?" His mother took off her glasses and rubbed her eyes. "That's right. You don't answer questions, you just ask them. *Was* that a question, by the way?"

He nodded.

"Perhaps the stations are saving the story for later. Sometimes they do that when they're waiting for more information." His mother paused. "Is this the sort of thing that the government might want to keep quiet?"

He shook his head.

"I'm sorry, Michael, but I'm not really in the mood to play Twenty Questions." She paused. "I've heard about computer viruses. That sort of thing always seems like a cruel prank, intelligent but not very smart. I hope that you aren't involved in anything like that."

"A virus? No." Too easy.

The solution came to him. Michael stood and ran his hand through his hair. "They're *suppressing* it."

He knew that the Finstater Foundation had money. Enough to fork out bribes? To how many people? For how long?

That was all right. He could be patient. Somebody was bound to talk. And talk. And talk. Argus would be destroyed. It just might take more time than he expected.

After all, it wasn't every day that a high school student was killed by an educational program.

"This is crazy!"

Ira had been working on his English homework when the phone rang. He held the receiver away from his ear. "Tess?"

As though it could be anyone else.

"If I interview Sandra this afternoon, then I have to interview the other candidates for student council, too." She paused. "Oh, god, I just realized. If your mother had picked up the phone, I would have yelled at her."

"That's right. Or at my father."

"I would have apologized, naturally. But they—he or she—would know who I wanted to talk to."

"Probably." He marked his page. "What time are you interviewing Sandra?"

"Noon." She paused. "Did you read that article I gave you?"

"I read it. You're saying that Argus is the great-great-grandmother of the holodeck."

"More than that. On the TV show, the holodeck was used as a game or for education. In reality, it would be an unpredictable narcotic. People could live their entire lives in dreams. This is frightening, Ira."

"It ain't gonna happen," he told her. Nothing. "Tess?"

"I'm not so sure," she said slowly.

2

"It's nice of you to see me on a Saturday," Tess said, as Sandra showed her into her bedroom.

The room had a pink ceiling and pink flowered wallpaper that matched the flounce on the four-poster bed. Stuffed animals sat on pink bookshelves, along with framed photos of Sandra taken at various proms.

Sandra waved her toward the desk, and Tess sat down on a pink chair. The other girl seemed to be waiting for her to say something. "Your room," Tess managed at last. "It's very pink."

To her relief, Sandra laughed. "My mom helped me decorate this room when I was ten. I'd like to change it, but my sister Caroline will move in when I leave for college. She loves it just the way it is. She's eight now."

Tess brought up several school issues. As she had expected, Sandra had a few pet topics and little knowledge about others. She talked about the ways in which the school was letting down teenage mothers. About additional funding for sports that might be better applied to programs for keeping students in school. "I suppose that won't win me any votes," she admitted ruefully.

"What about teenage suicides?" Tess had brought a list of questions. "What do you think the school should be doing in that respect?" She watched Sandra's face closely.

Not a blink. "The counselors have made it clear that they're available. The school paper always runs the phone number of the local crisis line. The subject of depression is covered in Biology and Health. To be perfectly honest, I don't see how much more they can do. I do have one suggestion, though. Last year the *Banner* ran an excellent series of articles on teenage suicides. Your editor might consider running it again."

Not a bad suggestion. Rerunning the articles would be a particularly good idea when student journalists had finals and little time to prepare new material.

The questions rolled on, and so did Sandra's answers. The school needed strong leadership. More students should take prominent roles which others could look up to. Tess might try putting her hair up. Had she tried it short?

Short. Tess looked up from her notepad. "Huh?"

Sandra was examining her critically. "You have great cheekbones, only they're hidden by all that hair."

Before she knew what was happening, Sandra had come

up to her and was holding her hair back. Tight. "Hey!" Tess yelped.

"That's better," Sandra said, looking at her and then releasing her hair. "You'd look good in curls, but I'm positive that you wouldn't feel comfortable. And if you don't feel comfortable with a look, it can't possibly suit you."

"Violence in our schools," Tess said weakly. "Are you for or against it?" She hadn't asked that, had she? She meant to ask for Sandra's opinion.

The blonde girl was doing something behind her head. "Violence can't be tolerated, of course. Anyone bringing a weapon to school is out. Fortunately, I've never heard of anything more serious at Banting than confiscated pocketknives. I hope we'll keep an atmosphere where that sort of situation doesn't occur."

For somebody who had never been interviewed, Tess thought, Sandra was handling the situation awfully well. She had also enabled Tess to read her notes more easily, since her hair was no longer falling forward onto her papers. "Are you positive that this is your first interview?"

"Well . . . my mom is president of the local pro-life society. I've been on hand when she was interviewed. She gets some really hard questions." Sandra reached into a drawer and took out an elastic band. She finished working behind Tess's head, then did something that involved pushing back a long strand at the front and pinning it near her ear. "There. Take a look at yourself in the mirror and see what you think."

Overcome with curiosity, Tess rose carefully and walked over to the three-way dresser mirror. "You braided it."

Sandra nodded. "This is something like a French braid.

It's simple to take care of—I know I don't like to spend time fooling with my hair in the morning. What do you think?"

Tess turned her head slowly. "It's not too bad." Lately she'd been getting increasingly aggravated by hair falling across her face. Once she even threatened to shave it all off. She turned her head the other way. This was okay.

"You'll need a trim to shape things up and to take care of those split ends." Sandra reached into her desk drawer and took out an address book. "I'll give you the number of my hairdresser. She doesn't charge a lot. Otherwise, we couldn't afford her."

In the mirror, one of Tess's eyebrows went up. Sandra's house was large and comfortable, located in what was commonly referred to as a "good" neighborhood.

"This is a family with four girls."

Meaning they could drop a major bundle each week with—she glanced at the business card Sandra handed her—Nicole the beautician. "Maybe I'll give her a call."

"She's also good when you want something fancy. Like for a dance."

Tess didn't comment. Years before, her mother had forced her to take dancing lessons. The experience had been painful for all concerned. The boys in class always wanted to dance with girls like Sandra.

The blonde girl was still fooling with her hair, folding the braid up on top of her head and holding it there. "Do you like Ira?" she asked.

Tess jerked. "Ouch!"

"I'm sorry. Did I pull your hair?"

"I moved." Her roots stung. "Why on earth would you ask that?"

"Well . . ." She stopped. "We're off the record, aren't we?"

"We can talk off the record," Tess said. "But you're way off base."

"Oh. That's too bad." From her expression, Sandra looked as though she actually thought it was too bad. "I think Ira likes me. That is, he *thinks* he likes me. He doesn't know me."

If Ira knew Sandra, Tess thought glumly, he'd be crazy about her. He was already crazy about her. He had gone through the Night Room for her after Graham met his worst nightmare.

"It's just that . . . oh, I don't know. In the waiting room, we had a lot of time on our hands. I couldn't help noticing how you were looking at him."

Tess's face was flaming. "Sometimes Ira irritates me, all right? He always has. That doesn't mean that I'm in love with him. Good grief."

"Okay, okay." Sandra backed off. "I didn't mean to upset you. He seems nice, that's all."

Tess grabbed up her notebook. "I think I have all I need. I'll phone you if I think of anything else." She headed toward the door. "Thanks for the hairstyle."

She practically ran from the house.

★   ★
★   ★
★   ★
3   ★

The phone rang again at Ira's house. This time there was silence. "Tess?"

"That was so embarrassing." He could barely hear her.

"So what happened? Did you find out anything?"

She cleared her throat, and her voice returned to normal. "I found out lots. Sandra doesn't care for pink anymore. She's wild about her boyfriend, although I'm sure you're disappointed to hear that. Oh, yes, her older sister had a child last year without being married. The whole family is supportive. Sandra knows an unplanned pregnancy doesn't mean the end of the world, just a crowded guest room. Her life is so rosy that I feel like throwing up. I've already brushed my teeth twice. And taken down my hair."

"Your hair?"

"Never mind. This whole thing is unutterably stupid. She's no more suicidal than I am." He wasn't expecting her laugh. "You know what this means, don't you? Patrick and Leanne probably ran into each other by accident. That means Mac and Leanne—"

He finished the sentence for her. "They don't have any reason to go out. Maybe I can find out what movie they're seeing. We could sit behind them and pretend to take notes."

He was asking her for a date. Sort of.

"Dumb," she said. "Very dumb."

On the other hand, maybe he wasn't.

He thought of something else. "What if Argus's information about Leanne and Patrick came from Leanne? Leanne took the tests, too. She could have told her interviewer that she was seeing Sandra's boyfriend. Maybe she wanted to talk about it to somebody. Maybe they've decided not to tell Sandra until after Christmas."

Tess didn't say anything for a minute. "I have another explanation. Mac said he saw something. He may even *think* he saw something. He told everybody, and that influenced the rest of you. Argus takes place in the mind, right?"

"Sort of." Tess hadn't gone through the Night Room. She didn't know how real it was. She might come up with all sorts of evidence that the program was crap, but he couldn't shake the nagging feeling that something was behind the prediction about Sandra.

"Let me guess," Tess said. "You want to find someone to go out with you on New Year's Eve, so you're hoping that Sandra and Patrick will break up. If you're right, you'll be first in line to ask her out."

"What are you doing on New Year's?" he asked casually.

"None of your business," she snapped.

She hung up on him.

* * *
* *
4 *

"Like you know anything," Mac said. It was 6:30 P.M. and Ira was phoning him with last-minute instructions. "Hey, I've gone out with girls before." Unlike some people.

"I don't know how to break this to you," Ira said, "but Leanne is a nice girl. You can't treat her like the other girls you know."

Ira made it sound like his normal approach was to throw a girl over his shoulder and head into the nearest cave. "Nice girl, huh?" Mac snorted. "And she's playing around with the guy who goes with her best friend." He had to remember that, just in case he started thinking she was *too* nice.

"A lot may be at stake here. You can't approach her like she's some football groupie."

This guy was definitely out of touch. "The team wasn't that great this year."

"No groupies?" Ira sounded disappointed. "What about the cheerleaders?"

"Get a life," Mac said. He hung up and then headed toward the door. He had already figured out on his own that Leanne was different from the other girls he knew. He was going to have to make conversation. Watch his language. Avoid fast moves.

Until he didn't have to.

SATURDAY, DECEMBER 9

5

The caroling rehearsal went as Joy had predicted. Most of the members of the church youth group had known each other a long time. There were cliques of girls who barely glanced at her. She was also introduced to a few kids who were relatively new to the area, some of them looking as ill at ease as she felt.

By the end of the evening, she had learned a few names, and a few people had learned her name. Another rehearsal would be held the following Saturday. The church bus really needed repairs, so she'd probably go.

She had learned that several carolers went to Banting. "That's good," her mother said when Joy told her. "Isn't it?"

Maybe it would have been good if it weren't for Argus. Thanks to her participation in an educational project, her most private dreams were doomed to become public knowledge.

She dreaded returning to school on Monday.

6

Michael knew now that he shouldn't have tried to take a look at his so-called victim, but curiosity had gotten the best of him. The previous Sunday, he had hung around outside her house, waiting until he spotted a teenager through the window. Then he rang the doorbell and pretended to have a wrong address.

He didn't know what he'd expected to find. She was a teenage girl, intelligent but not extraordinary. She was helpful, although wary of strangers. He had managed to see her twice since then, near bus stops. Not a good idea, but something kept drawing him toward her. The last time, he was sure that she had noticed him. If he didn't watch out, he'd find himself reported as a stalker.

Michael Radford—a stalker! The thought was ludicrous.

His initial plan had been to program in one heck of a nightmare. It would be simple enough to frighten someone to death, particularly if another part of the programming caused that individual to believe she had a bad heart. Simple or not, his plan had exceeded his comfort level.

And then he had remembered Bix.

His old golden retriever had been put down earlier that year. Bix had been almost blind, suffering from rheumatism.

Sometimes Michael sat with him while he spent his last days dreaming of runs through the woods, sides trembling, occasionally rising up to snap at phantom rabbits.

Perhaps there was no set of ethics to cover this situation, but he decided that a human being deserved at least as peaceful a death as an old dog. It would just take more work.

Time had been short when he finished modifying the program so it would conclude at a time of success for the individual taking part, whatever success might mean to that person. (The brain would provide details—it always did.) This success would be followed by a quick death, which was better than most people could count on.

He was still waiting for a news report, for some sort of leak. He'd even gone onto the campus and spoken with the few people hanging around the Computer department. Nothing. And he still hadn't slept.

He hadn't expected that seeing the girl would bother him so much.

Normally Ira would not phone another guy to ask how a date went, but this was different. This date was more like a group project. He waited until 9:00 A.M. before calling. "So, how did it go?" he asked.

Mac's voice was gravelly. "How did what go?" He sounded like he was just waking up.

"Last night. Leanne. You and Leanne. How did it go?"

"It *went*. What's the matter? You want the gory details?"

"No." Too quickly. "I mean, did you two get along okay?"

"Of course we got along okay."

A few details would be good. "So what did you do? Did you go somewhere?"

"We saw a western. It was all right. The night wasn't a total loss."

Not a total loss meant that not a whole lot happened between them, physically.

"Do you think she'll go out with you again?"

"Are you a girl?" Mac didn't wait for an answer. "Then stop talking like a girl. And don't ask stupid questions. Of course she will."

"You should call her today."

"What?"

"Today. Phone her." He waited for Mac to tell him that this was not the way things were done.

The phone slammed down. Yes!

Next Ira phoned Tess. "I think Mac and Leanne got along okay," he said cautiously. He reported their brief conversation.

"No macho bragging?"

"He said they went to a movie. If anything happened after that, he didn't tell me about it."

"I'm amazed." She paused. "By the way, I'm definitely going to write about Argus soon. I don't know whether Ms. Ruddley will approve, but people ought to know what can happen. In the case of Barbara, the prediction was just plain dumb. Graham was a mess afterward."

"We were warned that we might not like what we saw," Ira cut in. "Anyway, Graham is fine now. He says that the program was wrong. He says he'll make sure it was wrong. That's the idea behind Argus, remember?"

"Argus certainly isn't supposed to say that someone is dead. How is that supposed to help anyone?" She barely stopped for breath. "It just occurred to me—no one ever told me how Sandra was supposed to have died."

"Uh. Well, I asked you. In the future, I mean. I figured you'd know. You said she stopped living." Silence. "Other people said the same thing."

A swift intake of breath. " *'She died because she stopped living'?* Do you honestly think I'd ever say something like that? How about, 'She won the cooking prize because she prepared something'? Or, 'The tornado turned out to be a big wind'? I can't believe that you—that Barbara—went to so much trouble for a stupid thing like that." She began laughing. "I actually thought that there was reason for concern."

Maybe the whole thing really was dumb. "So, you're going to interview everyone?"

"And Karen Narita, if I can."

"Do you want to interview me?" he asked.

"Okay. It would be better if we talk in person."

"Today? How about getting together for lunch?"

$$* \quad * \quad *$$

2

At noon Tess picked him up in her VW. They headed to a tree-lined area of small shops and cafés located near the university. "Hey," Ira said as she parked, "we tried to do what's right."

"Oh, I'm sure that everybody did the right thing." She shoved her hands forcefully into woolen gloves. "I wouldn't have thought it possible to hate a computer program, but I'm beginning to take a real dislike to Argus. It's supposed to help people, not scare them." Her lips were tight. "I'm going to write a great story. Count on it."

They got out of the car. "Do you want to take a walk first?" he suggested.

"I want," she said, "to burrow through the pavement. I can't believe that I pursued this matter without getting more information." She gave him a slight smile. "A walk would be good." They started off. "Thanks, Ira."

"For what?" He was surprised.

"For being nice, I guess. Sandra's lucky. After all, you've only been trying to make sure she's all right."

An elderly woman was coming toward them with a shopping cart. As Ira pulled in closer to Tess in order to give her room to pass, their arms bumped slightly. "We've all been doing that, not just me."

"I'm investigating," Tess said stubbornly. "And I don't know if I'm even doing it well."

Even though the woman had passed, they continued to walk close together, staying that way as they crossed the street. It was Sunday, but most of the small stores were open. Their steps matched well. Ira had always been attracted to small females. Now he found that he liked having one who could keep up with him easily.

Tess stopped to look at a laptop computer displayed in a window. "I'm thinking of asking to take my turn after all. I'm still next in alphabetical order, and it isn't as though Argus doesn't have my data. Maybe I can crawl on my belly a little, ask to go in at the same time as Sandra."

"Don't," he said sharply.

She stopped. "Why not?"

She could find herself in a hotel room with Ira. Despite her bravado, he was positive that this was a girl who became embarrassed about personal matters. She might never speak to him again just to prove to Argus that it was wrong. "For the same reasons you dropped out," he hedged. "I read the holodeck article, remember? Not that I think it could happen."

"Why not?" she asked again.

Why did Tess have to ask so many questions? "Because that's not how people work." He fumbled for the right words. "I think that people need other people. Real people."

"A lot of people would be satisfied with a good imitation." She dug her hands into her pockets. "You definitely wouldn't see as many divorces. If you decided that you didn't like your wife anymore, you could delete her."

She obviously meant her comment seriously, but for some reason both started laughing.

They drifted on. "By the way," Tess said, "what kind of career did you have in the future?"

He hadn't even thought about that. "I don't know. The subject never came up."

"You're kidding."

"It didn't seem important." He had assumed that he was doing okay. His mom was a pharmacist. Chemistry was one of his strongest subjects, and he liked dealing with people. He'd probably do the same.

"One of the main purposes of Argus is to find out where your talents lie."

"I did."

She was waiting. They were still standing a few doors down from the computer shop. "So what is your main talent?"

"Loving."

Tess opened her mouth as though she were about to say something sarcastic. She didn't. "Loving," she echoed.

"I was a husband and father. A good family man. That's what I saw." He put his hand on her arm. "Are you ready for lunch now?"

"Lunch. Right." She seemed disoriented as she looked around. The restaurant was half a block away.

"Straight ahead." Ira barely noticed a blond young man coming out of a computer supply store with a small bag in his hand. Tess tensed up. She moved closer and put her hand through his arm.

"What's wrong?"

"Sorry," she apologized breathlessly. "There's a guy behind us. Don't laugh, but I think he's been following me." She was standing so near that he could feel her trembling. "He showed up at my door last week and said he had the wrong address. I'm positive that I've seen him a couple of times since."

"Has he ever said anything else?"

She shook her head. "It could just be a coincidence. Come on, let's walk faster."

Walk faster, hell. Ira stopped abruptly. Tess dropped his arm as he swung around to face the person walking behind them. College age was his first impression. Blond. Runt. Intense blue eyes in a pale face.

The guy stood there staring at Tess.

"Hey, buddy—" Ira started.

That was when he spoke to her. Two words that Ira didn't catch, but the expression on his face was one of utter joy. Then he turned and ran the other way, dropping his bag as he recovered his balance on an icy patch on the sidewalk.

"Hey!" Ira took off after him. "Wait!"

He had no idea what he planned to do once he caught him, except that he wanted to get to the bottom of this. This knight-errant stuff was habit-forming, and he wasn't about to have some crazy guy stalking Tess.

The guy took off toward the main street, maybe planning to get lost in the crowd of Christmas shoppers or to duck into a store. As he glanced back at a red light, his eyes met Ira's, and he abruptly darted into traffic.

Ira lost sight of him as car brakes squealed and people leaned on their horns. There was the sickening sound of an impact. Christ. "I never meant . . ." He never meant anything to happen. With others, he headed toward the accident.

"He ran out of nowhere," an upset woman motorist said, as several people knelt over the man lying on the pavement.

Someone called for assistance on a cellular phone. Two people knew first aid. A man began directing traffic. Someone brought a blanket.

Tess caught up. "I just wanted to talk to him," Ira said brokenly.

"It's not your fault." She slipped her hand into his. "It's not mine, either." He could hear a siren in the distance.

He held on to her. "What did he say to you?"

She told him. "What could it mean?"

Ira shook his head. "I don't know."

You're alive.

* *
* *
* *
3 *

"Take a seat over there," the harried-looking nurse said. "You may have a long wait."

Tess had found a charge slip inside the bag dropped by the injured man. His name was Michael Radford. "I don't know why I wanted to come here," she said as she and Ira took chairs in the emergency area. "It's not like I'll be allowed to speak with him. I wouldn't want to. But I need to know . . ." She stopped. "In a way, I'm almost glad you're with me." Her eyes didn't meet his.

No *in a way* for him. No *almost*. Nothing. Not one lame word came to his lips. Now that they had declared a cease-fire, he couldn't think of anything to say.

"I don't want him to be dead," she said.

"He won't die," Ira promised her. He wouldn't let this guy be dead. This guy had some explaining to do.

THE NIGHT ROOM

They had plenty of company. The area was busy with hospital personnel passing to and fro. People in wheelchairs sat patiently, waiting to be seen. "They might not even tell us anything," Ira said after they had been breathing hospital air for half an hour.

"You could leave," Tess said. He told her not to be dumb.

They had been sitting almost an hour when a young man wearing a gray sweatshirt and jeans charged through the door. Everybody in the waiting area looked up as he headed toward the desk. "I'm Dave Radford. My kid brother is here. They said he was hit by a car." He looked like a slightly older, taller, and darker version of the accident victim.

The nurse told him to wait. He took one of the vacant chairs. Ira and Tess both rose, setting down their magazines. "Is your brother Michael Radford?" Tess asked. "We saw the accident. He dropped this." She held out the bag.

"Computer disks." Dave gave a harsh laugh. "That's Mike, all right. A computer nut. You saw Mike get hit?"

"He's been following her for a week," Ira said.

"That's crazy!" His voice rose.

"Maybe not following me." Tess spoke calmly. "But I've seen him several times watching me." She told him about the person who came to her door. "I'm sure it was him. His eyes—" She swallowed. "I hope he's all right. But I need to know if he's dangerous. And I want him to know that he has to stop."

"Mike? Dangerous?" Dave stared at her incredulously.

"Hey, when he gets into a project, he's obsessive. But he is not nuts." He looked at her more closely. "Are you a friend of Sara?"

"Who's Sara?" Tess asked blankly.

"His girlfriend. Ex-girlfriend. They broke up last month. Okay, maybe that's not the connection. What about computers?"

"I have a computer," Tess answered.

"Are you an expert?" the brother asked. "Mike's really gung ho. He almost never takes time out."

Tess shook her head. "I'm far from being an expert. I'm a high school student. I'm on the school paper."

"I can't see Mike having any connection with a high school newspaper. This is nuts."

"So what does it mean?" Tess asked Ira when they left the hospital. Another hour had passed.

"It means—I don't have a clue what it means."

Michael's brother was finally allowed to see him. When Dave came out, he spoke to them briefly. Michael had muttered something before he lapsed into unconsciousness, repeated it several times. He wasn't even sure what Michael was saying, something about *the sixth person* or *six*. Maybe he was trying to say that he felt sick.

Michael Radford would recover, but he was in for a long stay.

Tess put her fingertips to her forehead as soon as they were outside. "Why has he been following me—a computer whiz I've never met?"

"He's a nutcase," Ira said loudly. "You'll go home. You'll tell your parents. You'll talk to the cops."

"He never threatened me," Tess said at last. "Never. He just said that I was alive, and he seemed surprised. Glad." She turned to face him. "Why, Ira?"

4

Dr. Halstrom's flight had been delayed. She had arrived home two hours later than expected, and now she was exhausted. The speech had gone well except for too many foolish questions from the audience. She always had difficulty hiding her impatience.

She went to the refrigerator and poured herself a glass of wine, then returned to the couch and took a photograph from the lamp table. It was identical to the one in her office, showing two embracing skiers. The last photograph. "So, Rolfe," she said to the man in red. "This is good. There is a great deal of interest in the project."

No reply. She traced his outline with the tip of her little finger. "You would be proud."

Sighing, she leaned back and closed her eyes. They had

both been so young on that day that began so beautifully and ended so badly. They had been skiing.

She could see Rolfe a short distance away, tall and handsome. He was laughing. "Ursula, come on. Let's race back to the lodge."

She had just started off when it happened. A small noise, like a distant rifle shot. And then the avalanche swept toward her in a terrible coda. Nothing could be heard over the roar. A scream stuck in her throat as she tried to look back for Rolfe, who was a strong skier but not as strong as she was. (She had won medals, while he simply enjoyed.) And then the sudden darkness, blocking out the sun, blocking all noise so she could not hear her own bones snapping like twigs. Could not hear whether Rolfe called her name with his last breath as she tried to call his.

She had always known that Rolfe's family was wealthy. He spent money easily and well, but never lavishly. After his death, after she learned that she would never ski again— perhaps never walk—she was shocked again when she learned the value of his estate. He had named her as his heir. From that point, her way was clear. She set up the Rolfe Finstater Foundation and began to develop Argus.

Her background in psychology held her in good stead. Also, from the time she was a child, her father had taught her about computers. It took nearly ten years before she found Rolfe again. At first he was no more than a transparent image of himself, always wondering why she wept when she saw him. Then he took on life of his own.

When her father discovered the focus of her research, he had approached her in his usual calm, sensible way. *"You have a morbid preoccupation with death. Life is for the living, Ursula.*" Ursula had closed the door on her family.

One of the first things she did with Argus was reconstruct the avalanche to see if there was any way that she could have saved Rolfe. No. She had run the program over and over, felt her bones snap over and over. There had been no warning. Perhaps the birds were quieter than usual, and then one had chirped. By the time a small cracking sound alerted her that something was wrong, it was already too late. If she had not turned to find that small red figure in all the whiteness, she might have saved herself.

And yet—not to turn would have been unthinkable.

As she continued her research, she developed other programs about their future together. In these programs, they married and grew older together. Three children were born, two girls and one boy. Their son was studying medicine, no trouble at all. The older girl played the piano brilliantly and looked out at the stars. Rolfe said she and Greta were alike.

The younger daughter was Rolfe's favorite, although Dr. Halstrom often found her high spirits irritating. Lately this teenage daughter had been getting into scrapes with wild boys.

Her children lived in a drawer.

These programs were personal, of course. Now that her preliminary research was complete, many institutions were expressing interest. She turned away all would-be investors. Argus was not only for those who could afford it. Argus would be given freely to everyone.

In the technically developed world, at least, everyone

could have a life without want. Success would be given to all—not the success of the soul that the religious people promised, but success in this life. The school version did exactly as it should, showing individual flaws that might be mended. It also created an appetite for Argus's real purpose. If life itself did not turn out well, Argus could fill in the empty spaces. There would be love, for everyone. All the love that you could hold to you with both hands.

And it would never, ever, end.

Joy stood on the concrete steps leading into Banting High, preparing herself for total humiliation. She hadn't been thinking straight when she pretended to be sick on Friday morning. Instead she should have gone to school and asked the others not to say anything about seeing her as the ultimate starlet. Now it was too late. The doors loomed wide before her.

So okay, she decided. She wouldn't apologize for saying that she wanted to be an actress. She also wasn't going to deny that she was on a diet, because she was, to lose fifteen pounds. It was one thing to want to look and feel better, another to become a human Barbie doll. She was no more responsible for Argus's vision than she would be for the content of a movie she chose to watch.

Other students were pushing past her. She took a deep breath and went in. As she came into the busy hallway, she waited for the first laugh, for the first pointed finger. The first exaggeratedly jutting chest.

Nothing happened. No one glanced in her direction as she went down the hall toward her locker. Joy didn't know very many people, but after the play several students had congratulated her on her performance. They must recognize her.

Something occurred to her. Maybe *everybody* in her Health class had missed school on Friday out of embarrassment. Maybe it wasn't too late.

To her relief, she spotted Barbara right away. They had never really spoken, but Joy didn't think she was a mean person. She hurried to her side. "About the other night . . . has anybody said anything? About the way I looked, I mean?"

At first the other girl's expression was blank. Then comprehension dawned. "I don't think so." Her smile was conspiratorial. "The program was sort of ridiculous in places, wasn't it? I'll tell you what. You don't tell people how I looked, and I won't tell about you."

"Okay." Joy felt much better. She could see how Barbara might feel embarrassed about being shown as pregnant. "I won't say a word."

"If you ask me," Graham told Joy, "the whole thing is a bunch of bull."

"It was kind of dumb. It was interesting, though. Some things seemed correct . . . a little."

Graham was frowning. "For me, it was just plain wrong."

"But that's the idea behind Argus. We're supposed to say *that's me* or *that's not going to be me*."

"That is not going to be me," Graham said heavily. He shrugged. "Maybe someday I'll see what the new version of Argus is like."

"Maybe."

Mac was the only one she feared. She caught up with him after first period. "About Thursday, at the university—"

He stopped. "Are you okay now?"

Her face warmed. "I talked to Ms. Ruddley before I left. Mac, have you told anybody about it? About me, I mean?" She didn't see how he could resist.

"About you blubbering in the hall? Why should I?"

"Not that. In the Night Room, at the reunion."

"I never saw you," he said at last. "I got sort of tied up talking to people. That party was a blast."

She opened her mouth to protest. He had asked her out. Then she remembered one of Ms. Ruddley's warnings. They would all appear at the same party, but they would each have different experiences. Mac might not have recognized her.

The buzzer sounded. "Gotta go," he said.

She and Ira had second period together. She went up to his desk before class. "Hi." Repeated telling wasn't making this any easier. "About Thursday—the way I looked—I'd appreciate your not telling anybody—if you haven't already."

"Did you see me at the party?" he asked.

She nodded. It wasn't as though he had lost his hair on purpose.

"Look," he said, "if that story gets around, I get dumb remarks for a few days. I can take it, if I have to. I don't think that anybody from our class is talking about the others. I haven't said anything about you. I won't."

"I've already spoken with Tess. That leaves Sandra." She began to turn away.

"Sandra's turn was postponed. She's going this afternoon."

"I'll try to find her at lunchtime." Right now Joy knew more about Sandra's possible future than Sandra herself.

For maximum value, those who enter early are asked to refrain from discussing their insights with others waiting.

She wouldn't say a word.

2

Mac had thought about calling Leanne on Sunday—for maybe three seconds. No way. Leanne knew the rules as well as he did. Instead, he managed to run into her in the hall before third period. After they both said things about how the movie had been good, he asked her, "So, you want to go for a drive or something after school?"

"I'm sorry," Leanne replied with what sounded like real regret. "My folks prefer that I don't go out during the week. I'm supposed to study."

"My old man doesn't keep after me that way," Mac said. Something occurred to him. "Thursday's a school night."

She smiled. "So are Monday, Tuesday, and Wednesday. Sunday is a school night, but my parents don't mind my going out if I'm caught up."

He had seen her with Patrick on Thursday. "Argus was last Thursday."

"Was it? Oh, that's right. Sandra is having her turn today. She's really excited."

Something was wrong. Leanne had gone out with Patrick on Thursday night. Mac had seen them together. Now she was telling him that she never dated on school nights.

So, what do you call last Thursday? He couldn't ask that. If a girl asked him to account for his time, he'd figure she was possessive. That kind of thing rang alarm bells.

Maybe she had forgotten that Mac had been at the White Spot. Or maybe she was lying to him in that way girls did when they wanted to spare your feelings. She was saying that her folks didn't allow her to go out during the week. Then, when—if—he asked about the weekend, she'd be busy.

Maybe you could give me a call next month.

As if.

"I told Sandra about you," Leanne said almost shyly. "That is, I told her that we had a good time Saturday."

"Yeah?" He was barely listening.

"If you're interested in doing something this weekend, Sandra suggested that the four of us might go out. Not Friday, though. Patrick's last final is Friday, and I think they want to go out alone that night to celebrate."

"Wait." This was definitely coming through. "You're talking about you and me, and Patrick and Sandra." She nodded. "The four of us."

"That's right."

And Thursday was a school night, when she wasn't supposed to date. "Patrick. He's the guy you were with at the restaurant, right? Last Thursday?"

That's when she told him a few things about the reason she was out with Patrick. "This is a secret, of course."

"Son of a—!" Now it all made sense. Mac told her about a few things: about what Argus had said about Sandra; about their following her and Patrick.

"You're crazy," Leanne said flatly. "You're all crazy."

After that, he got her to agree to meet them at lunchtime. He rounded up Ira and Tess and Barbara, told them to be in the cafeteria at the table in the far corner.

"Okay," he said as he and Leanne sat down. "You all know Leanne." An uncomfortable-looking group of students murmured their greetings. "I found out why Leanne and Patrick were out on Thursday night."

"I was helping Patrick to shop for Sandra's Christmas present." Leanne seemed annoyed. "It's supposed to be a surprise, but if you must know, he's getting her a pre-engagement ring."

"It's like they'll be engaged to be engaged," Mac explained helpfully. To him, it sounded like Patrick was getting ready to make some kind of advanced move on Sandra.

"He wanted advice on the sort of ring she might like. Also, Sandra and I have the same ring size, so I was trying them on." She surveyed the table. "You didn't really think that I would go out with the boyfriend of my best friend?"

Mac saw Ira give a little jump as though one of the girls had kicked him under the table. Tess, probably.

"Some girls might." Barbara's cheeks were red.

"Well, I'm not one of them." Leanne's frown faded slightly. "Did Argus really say that Sandra was dead?"

Ira, Mac, and Barbara all nodded.

"And that she was suicidal?"

Another chorus of nods.

Leanne was looking at one face after the other. "Sandra is not suicidal. She's the least suicidal person I've ever met."

"How's her health?" Ira asked.

"Sandra spent August working as a camp counselor. She had a complete physical examination beforehand. She was a lifeguard, for heaven's sake."

Stunned silence. Mac was really enjoying this.

Tess shook herself slightly. "It will make a great story, that's for sure."

"This from the girl who didn't bother to take her turn," Mac said to Leanne.

Uh-oh. Leanne was looking at him as though he was a complete stranger, and one she didn't particularly want to know. She stood up with her books. "Anyway, now you know that you were completely wrong about Sandra."

Mac stood, too. "Where are you going?"

"Library." She strode off.

He caught up with her a few tables away. "So, what about Friday?" he asked. "Do you want to hit another movie or what?"

Her eyes were cool. "You still want to?"

"Sure."

"But you wouldn't have asked me out in the first place if it wasn't for Argus, would you?"

Mac couldn't see what one thing had to do with the other. "So what? We had a good time, didn't we?"

At last she nodded. "All right. Besides, you were trying to save the life of my best friend. I can't fault you for that."

He was a good guy. That was worth points. "I'm not really into that doubling stuff."

"We'll see what's playing on the weekend," she said. She began to turn away, then stopped. "On Saturday, were you on your best behavior?"

"Huh?" Like he didn't know what she meant.

"Never mind. I suppose I'll find out."

Yes, ma'am. Beaming, Mac returned to the table. He sat down. "She's crazy about me," he announced.

"All's well that ends well," Barbara said. "Personally, I'm mortified."

"Too bad Ms. Ruddley isn't back," Tess said. "She'll probably try to shut down the entire program."

Ira crumpled up his milk carton. "Argus only shows what might be, not what will be."

Something occurred to Mac. "What's going to happen to Sandra today when she takes her turn?"

"Maybe it works like the post office," Barbara suggested. "No one at this address—return to sender."

"Better than the dead letter office," Tess muttered.

They all fell silent. Mac was the only one who finished his lunch, although he helped both Tess and Barbara to polish off theirs.

He was doing great.

3

"Ira, wait."

School had just ended, and Ira was about to head toward his car. He turned to see Sandra heading toward him. She had said his name, and no bells rang.

"Hi, Sandra." Nothing. She was an attractive girl, and that was all. Somewhere, in his effort to save her life, she had lost her magic.

"I think we should talk," she said.

Maybe there was still a small glow. He supposed that a bit of glitter had to cling to someone who had occupied so many of his waking thoughts. As she looked up at him, she had the smile of a fond aunt. "Leanne told me about Argus," she said. "About what all of you did."

He waited for her to offer her thanks. *Aw, shucks.*

"You should have told me."

He almost laughed. "We kept hoping that Ms. Ruddley would get back." Would they have told Sandra eventually? He had no idea.

She did thank him then. "The whole thing is so ridiculous. How could anyone think that I would kill myself?"

Like people who killed themselves belonged to an exclusive club. "Anybody can commit suicide." It was as simple as that. "Skip it." He glanced up at the wall clock. "I thought Leanne said your appointment was right after school."

"I canceled," she said. "There didn't seem any point. I talked to Tess. She's writing a news story about Argus, did you know that?" She didn't wait for his answer. "Tess is taking my turn this afternoon. She phoned and they agreed to reinstate her. She wants to see for herself what Argus is like. It has something to do with being a reporter." She lowered her voice. "She likes you."

And their kids were Carl and Bob. He knew all about that.

Joy was coming toward them. "Don't you have your turn this afternoon?" she called to Sandra.

"Joy doesn't know about the suicide thing," Ira told Sandra under his breath.

Sandra nodded. "I decided not to go after all," she said smoothly. "I heard that my prediction wasn't very good."

Joy's eyes widened. "Nobody was supposed to tell."

"Somebody did," Ira said.

Sandra shifted her books in her arms. "It didn't sound like any sort of future I'd want to see."

"But why?" Joy was plainly bewildered. "You were there with your boyfriend. I mean, he was your husband. Patrick, right? You both looked happy together. You showed me the pictures of your three little ones. And you were so excited about the work you were doing."

"Wait," Ira whispered. Sandra was staring at him. "You can't have seen Sandra at the party."

"I did. I located everybody except Tess. I thought I saw her, but it turned out to be someone else." She turned back to Sandra. "Really, I wouldn't mind that kind of future."

For a second the thought ran through his mind that Joy was faking the whole thing. No, she knew that he had been balding. "What did Barbara look like?" he asked.

"I didn't talk to her, but I saw her sitting with a man who was really handsome. She was wearing a green dress. Emerald. She was pregnant."

"Pregnant?" Sandra echoed. "This is all getting too strange. I thought Argus was supposed to be scientific." She reached into her purse for her car keys. "I am so glad that I canceled my turn. Anyway, I'll see you both in class tomorrow."

Ira watched as she left. The last bits of glitter sparkled on the hall floor where she had stood, then blinked out.

"Somebody said that Barbara designed sportswear." Joy looked like her head ached. "Um . . . your wife wanted my autograph." Ira winced. Someone else had seen him with Tess. "She seemed nice. I felt bad because she was a nutritionist, and she wanted to talk about a diet I was supposed to recommend. And of course I didn't know—"

Her words struck him. "What did you say?"

"Your wife? She was a dietitian. You said she worked at a hospital."

"Wait." This didn't make sense. In the future he saw, Tess was a reporter. "Describe my wife."

Joy looked uncomfortable. "Her hair was short. Blonde."

"The hell it was!" Ira yelled. As other students glanced in their direction, he lowered his voice. "I'm sorry, but this is important. You said you spoke with Sandra—actually spoke with her." Joy nodded miserably. "And you talked to my wife, who was blonde. My wife was not blonde. She wasn't."

He took a few other details from her. Graham had been drinking. Check. Graham's wife. Check. Mac had been too friendly (blush). "I really have to go," Joy said at last. "My mom is picking me up."

He located Barbara in the school library. "Nothing makes sense," he said after the librarian ejected them into the hall for talking too loudly. "Computers are supposed to make sense."

"Wait," Barbara said. "Argus uses variables—data from our personal information—to calculate its results. We are only supposed to see the results, and we're all supposed to see the same things. Joy was the first to go in. She saw most of the same things that we did . . . but not all." She shook her head. "The results shifted after Joy's turn. In order for that to happen, there must have been a truly major change in the program code. But what?"

An explanation was coming to Ira, simple and horrible. He thought of the man who had followed Tess, his words when he saw her. *"You're alive!"* Number six.

"Maybe death is just another variable to Argus," Ira said slowly.

She stared at him. "What are you saying?"

"Tess has to be the key." He pulled the original announcement from his notebook. "Look—Tess was the original number six. She was still in the program when Joy took her turn, and that's when Joy saw Sandra." More important, she had seen Ira married to some blonde. "When Tess dropped out, she must have triggered something in the code. *Sandra* became number six."

He had been feeling calm, but now the skin on his face was drawing back and tightening like he was getting ready to scream. "That's how Argus knew that Sandra was going to die. I don't know how or why, but Argus is programmed to make the sixth person commit suicide."

"Not suicide." Barbara grabbed his arm. "At the party, nobody knew how Sandra killed herself. If it were suicide, she would have gotten exact instructions. Everybody would know the details, like—" Like a short walk off a high building. She swallowed. "Instead, they described a system shutdown."

Emergency equipment had been in the room, a hospital a couple of blocks away, and their parents had to sign all those release forms. But everything was supposed to be okay.

Ira gaped. "You're saying that Argus could murder somebody?"

"We don't know what Argus can do. Up to this time, there has never been anything like it. Ira," Barbara said urgently, "Tess is on her way there now. Her appointment is in less than twenty minutes."

* *
*   *
*   *
4   *

The telephone number of the Finstater Foundation was on the pamphlet they had been given. Ira headed toward an unoccupied pay phone at the end of the hall. It rang once . . . twice.

Come on, Ira prayed. *Be there, somebody.*

He must have been blind not to see it before. Sandra's death had been given as hard information. Argus had done the best it could with the information it had been fed.

"Rolfe Finstater Foundation."

Thank God. "Look," he said, "a girl is coming in there."

The voice droned on. "No one is available to speak with you, but if you will leave your name . . ."

"It's a recording." He was about to slam down the receiver when Barbara stopped him.

"Leave a message, Ira. They might check." They might also both be in the control booth right now while the lights dimmed.

He left a brief message. "Dr. Halstrom—Karen—Tess Norville has an appointment. The program has been tampered with. Argus may be dangerous. She must not take her turn." Then he hung up. "I have to get over there." He dug out his keys with shaking hands. "I need gas. Maybe I have enough." There was no time to fill up.

Barbara didn't drive. "I'll stay here," she told him. "I'll try to contact my parents. Or someone else at the university who might understand." That was another thing about Hell Week—the university was not fully staffed.

The university wasn't far. He thought of calling 911. The problem was that this was so complicated, he would waste precious time giving the necessary background. Tess might be dead by the time he managed to convince anyone of the seriousness of his concerns.

He hurried down the hall.

"Good luck!" Barbara called after him.

Ira's teeth were clenched tightly as he took the fastest route to the university. It was located in a suburb, and traffic was increasing because of a combination of Christmas shoppers and the early rush hour. He didn't know the exact time of Tess's appointment. Maybe Dr. Halstrom had started early and she was already lying dead in that black room.

Argus had been treating them as though they were all characters in a glorified Nintendo game. The difference was that instead of palace guards being killed, the target was one teenage girl.

Ira's character had been designated as the marrying kind, so of course he had to have a wife. Even if he and Tess were perfect for each other, they couldn't very well get married if she died in high school. No Tess? No problem. Argus could provide a new wife as easily as a new palace guard.

A black sedan cut in front of him, and he let out a string of curses. The driver flipped him the bird. He didn't have time for that kind of crap. He tried to relax, but all he could see was Tess lying there, eyes wide, as she stared at her last nightmare.

"She is not a variable!" he yelled.

"I've read as much as I could find about Argus," Tess said as she walked into the Night Room. She was nervous, and she didn't want to be nervous.

"Would you like to sit down now?" Karen asked.

"Oh. Sure." She hesitated. "It was kind of Dr. Halstrom to let me have a second chance." Now she was kissing up. She knew it. Chances were that the scientist was chuckling behind the one-way glass.

Karen lifted up the strap that was to go across her chest. "You remember this, don't you?"

Tess tried not to shiver. She stood there. "I want to loosen my belt. We're not supposed to wear anything constricting, right?" She had worn ordinary clothes to school, jeans, sweatshirt, khaki jacket.

"Perhaps you should remove your belt altogether," Karen suggested. "It's best if you're comfortable."

Slowly Tess slid the belt out of its loops and sat down. She tried to keep her mind disassociated as the assistant began fastening the straps that would bind her to the chair. Tess was a reporter. Her job was to remain calm, to take mental notes as things happened to her. She concentrated on staying detached, then thought of something that she really didn't want to make part of any newspaper story. "Karen?"

"What?"

"The interviewer asked questions about, well, romantic

things. I think I mentioned somebody's name. I mean, the name of a boy in my class popped into my head. I don't know why." She thought she saw a small smile on the other woman's lips.

"Yes?"

"I'm just saying—" She swallowed. "I don't think I'll ever get married. So, if Argus shows anything like that, Argus will be wrong. Right?"

"Argus only identifies patterns of behavior." Karen sounded as though she was reciting from a textbook. "Argus does not read the future."

"I know." She tried to find the words. "But how would you feel if you loved somebody and he wasn't there?"

She sounded like Juliet Capulet—a teenager dying of love.

Silence.

"You can still decide not to take part," Karen answered at last. "In fact, if you have difficulty distinguishing this program from reality, we encourage you to consider whether you wish to take part. Argus isn't for everyone."

"I understand," Tess said. "I really understand."

She did, too. Argus was a program still in its chrysalis stage. Some of its conclusions were valid, some absurd. The question was whether it could do real harm. That was the approach she planned to take in her story.

Ira would be at the reunion. Yes, she knew that he would be balding, but he'd also be older. He might actually look good that way. Some men did. She had to steel herself against being introduced to his wife and hearing about their wonderful family.

"Are you comfortable?" Karen asked as she finished fastening the straps.

A tear trickled from the corner of Tess's left eye, although she couldn't say why. She couldn't reach up and brush it away, so she felt it dissolve into her hair. "I'm fine."

"I think you need a bit more time to relax. I'll go out for a while and leave you here while the lights dim. Then I'll come back to introduce you to Argus. All right?"

"Is this your coffee break?" Tess asked.

"Tea." She started toward the door. "I'll be in the next room with Dr. Halstrom."

"Okay." As the assistant left, Tess wiggled her feet in the loose slippers. *Ira*, she prayed. *I want to see Ira.*

She did not believe. She was there only as a reporter.

Miraculously, Ira didn't hit any snags in traffic . . . until he was inside the university grounds. The roads narrowed past the playing fields, with patches of ice at the edges. A van had slid into a ditch, and a narrow two-lane road became a one-lane road with cars directed around the accident. The flow slowed to a crawl and then stopped altogether near the high-rise dormitories.

From where he was sitting, tapping on the steering wheel, he could see the observatory. Argus was housed in the next building. The road meandered around, and at the rate traffic was going, he could reach the lab faster on foot. Ira opened the door and stepped out into the cold winter day. The driver of the car behind his rolled down his window. "What in hell are you doing?"

The grass gave him good traction as he took off in the

direction of the lab. Behind him, car horns blasted. Ice crystals formed and defrosted in his lungs as he dashed through clouds of his own breath. At one point he hit a slick area and went down. He was up again immediately. He'd twisted his ankle, but he was too close to slow down now.

"Is that it?" Tess asked. "Argus?"

"Yes. Do you want to look inside the helmet?"

Tess nodded, difficult since the chair was tilted backward and she was feeling sleepy. The inside was smooth, except for what appeared to be metal buttons. "Thanks."

She wouldn't have thought that she could be hypnotized, but she was fairly sure it was happening. She felt pleasantly drowsy. She'd remember that.

"Raise up a little."

She did, and Karen put the helmet on her head. "It's not heavy at all." She didn't know why she was surprised. Everything computer-related was light these days.

The assistant adjusted the helmet. "Is that all right?"

She tried to nod again, but Argus made her head feel stiff and fastened in one position. " 's fine."

She wondered if the others had felt as she did. Apprehensive, but excited, too. Like she was about to step over the doorstep to something wonderful.

She heard butterfly wings. "Ira—"

"You can't go in there!" Karen yelled from the office.

An older woman was behind her. "Stop, or I call Security."

"Great," Ira hollered. "You call Security."

He limped through the doors, passing Tess's shoes. It was like entering Sleeping Beauty's castle, except that S.B. didn't wear a blue helmet on her head. He did the first thing he could think of, flicking on the light switches, then headed toward the chair to pull off the helmet. "Tess! Wake up!"

"Young man, get out!"

That was all? Butterflies? Someone was fumbling with the straps that bound her. "Ira? What—" Tess winced as she opened her eyes on a shatteringly bright room. "Is it over?"

"You're alive." Ira hauled her to a sitting position that made her head pound. To keep her balance, she held on to him. This was the second time in two days that someone had noticed that she was alive, as if it was some kind of miracle.

"You are in great difficulty, young man." Behind Ira stood Dr. Halstrom.

"Is this Ira?" Karen asked.

"Huh?" Ira said.

"He's in my class." Something else was happening besides the terrible headache. Her stomach churned. "I think I'm going to be sick."

Wordlessly, Karen handed her a small container.

"Why, Ira?" Tess asked weakly.

He tried to explain, tried to be clear. Okay, the whole thing was fantastic. That was the problem they'd been grappling with all weekend. Dr. Halstrom glowered at him. Tess sat there, clutching the container and taking deep breaths. The assistant seemed unsure, glancing back and forth from him to Dr. Halstrom. "There could be something in what he says," Karen said at last.

"Nonsense," Dr. Halstrom maintained. "Do you think I wouldn't know if someone had tampered with Argus?" She sucked in her breath. "Of course. This is the little girl from the high school newspaper. I understand now. She wants to write a terrible story."

"Not this badly." Tess retched into the cup. "I'm going to kill you, Ira," she gasped.

Two security officers came in. "Someone called to report a disturbance?"

Ira could see emotions warring in Dr. Halstrom's eyes. If the security officers questioned them, he and Tess would report the truth. The scientist obviously did not want any rumors spread that might harm her precious Argus.

"Perhaps a misunderstanding," she said. "A boy who did not want his girlfriend to take part."

"Great," one guard said. "I leave the police force and I still wind up with domestic disturbances."

Ira waited for the guards to leave before he said anything. "Don't let anybody go through Argus until you have your system checked out."

Dr. Halstrom was looking at Tess with real dislike. "Is that what you say, too, newspaper girl?"

Tess was still breathing deeply. "Three people saw evidence that Sandra died," she managed at last. "I didn't come here because—I didn't think—I was curious—"

"Are you saying that you do not plan to write about Argus?"

Her head went up "Of course I do. The program concerns students. It may be dangerous."

"Check out your system," Ira pleaded. He helped Tess out of the chair. "Barbara is phoning her parents," he told her

Tess moaned softly and clutched at him. "My head."

"Hang on to me."

"I may throw up on you." She staggered slightly.

"Steady." Ira put both arms around her, and she leaned against him. "Better?"

"Much better." They stood there for a few moments. When Tess spoke, her voice was muffled. "Right now you're just something to hold on to. Don't take this personally, okay?"

"Not me." He began to help her toward the hall.

When they reached the doorway, Tess looked back at the Night Room. Karen was replacing the blue helmet into its drawer, the scientist staring toward the blackened windows. "Now I'll never know. I'll never know what I would have seen."

"You'll just have to wait and find out for yourself." Ira squeezed her hand. "I think that you're going to enjoy your future. In fact, I give you my personal guarantee."

"That's very reassuring," Tess said.

He looked at her to see if she was being sarcastic. Maybe, but she also seemed shy. She let him help her out into the hallway, and the door to the Night Room clicked shut behind them.

* * *
*   *   *

5

Dr. Halstrom's hands were shaking as she sat at her desk. Those children. Those bad children wanted to destroy Argus. She had built the project for them, for all the children she would never have, to keep them from disappointment. And this was how they turned on her.

She looked up when she heard footsteps near the door. Karen stood there. "Dr. Halstrom, are you all right?"

"Another headache. I'll take a tablet. The girl—all right, I admit it. She upset me." Dr. Halstrom snorted derisively. "Reporters. Even the babies have sharp teeth."

"Still, there might be something to this."

Of course there might be something. There would be no point in spreading a rumor if the details sounded incredible. The girl could have claimed that an alien life form was attempting to collect brains through Argus. Instead, she decided on a hacker. A bogeyman. "I've run preliminary tests to determine interference. Nothing."

Soon the story would be all over the campus. All over—everywhere. Argus could not stand scrutiny that was too close. She had placed in the program an impulse for the user to return. Even though this impulse was felt as a mild tickle of curiosity, many people would find it unacceptable.

"Universal success," she said. "Is it such a terrible concept?" Dr. Halstrom drummed her fingers on the edge of her keyboard. "What shall we do now? What shall we do?" She was not asking Karen, and Karen wisely did not attempt to answer.

"Shall I cancel the appointments for tomorrow?" she asked.

"Not yet." Dr. Halstrom turned back toward the screen. "You might as well leave for the day."

"I don't mind staying—" Karen's voice broke off. "Really, I don't."

"No, go and find that nice young man of yours. Enjoy yourself. Consider that school is out for the day."

Karen hesitated. "What about you?"

"Me? I will think about ways to counteract these lies."

The assistant still had not moved from the doorway. "Perhaps you should bring in a company specializing in security breaches. That might dispel rumors."

As though an outside company would know more than she herself, she who had nursed Argus since its inception. "Perhaps," she echoed. She forced a tired smile. "Go on. Shoo. I believe that a half hour of sunshine remains. Go play."

At last the assistant took her coat from the rack behind the door. "Please phone me at home if you want anything."

"Of course," Dr. Halstrom answered, but her eyes were already fixed on the screen.

"So, Rolfe. So." Security had never been her strong point. Computer knowledge had grown immensely at the same time that she was narrowing down her research. She tried to envision a young computer genius, a clever boy who wished to kill in a clever way. Could it be true?

Perhaps. She could only imagine why he was doing this. At first she had thought Michael Radford must be a university student who had gone through Argus and didn't like his future. *Boo hoo, I will kill your program and my future will be dead, too.* She had checked Argus's records and his name did not appear. However, she discovered him in the profile of a girl who had been through in November. Sara Jannings. She brought up the notes about him taken by Sara's interviewer.

Ah. Michael was brilliant. Not so tall (so he might try harder). Destructive. Punishing, like others that the girl found attractive. Argus would have seized this pattern.

The public purpose of the program was to encourage students to take their lives into their own hands. Perhaps the girl had acted. Poof, the boy had no girlfriend.

The irony was that Dr. Halstrom was close to making public the so-called Argus II (there was only one Argus, but she had known that she would have to introduce her real purpose carefully). If Michael wanted this girl so badly, he would only have to come to the Finstater Foundation. He could have his Sara as Dr. Halstrom had Rolfe, now and through all eternity.

She sat there as late afternoon became night, thinking of methods of damage control. This was merely a setback, a small thing. Nothing had actually happened. Some teenagers had become overexcited. They let their imaginations run away with them.

The Foundation would tighten its security; the rumors would eventually die away. Perhaps whispers of danger would even create additional interest in the project.

Perhaps the truth would come out.

Her headache had returned. She felt ill and older than her years. Frail—she who had always despised weakness.

Rolfe would comfort her. His soothing presence would allow her to relax so she could deal with this catastrophe. Dr. Halstrom took out the box of orange disks and laid it on her desk.

She smoked a last cigarette, smoked it all the way until her fingertips felt the warmth of the glowing tip. She needed to decide on a disk for this winter night. An evening without crises would be nice. She was on edge and in no mood for more excitable children. The younger daughter could stay out with her current motorcycle playmate.

Over the years she had found that she preferred the programs she referred to as "the little days." These were ordinary times of work and relaxation with her husband. One or the other would prepare a meal. They would sit quietly and talk over glasses of wine, perhaps listen to an opera recording.

She selected a quiet spring evening with Rolfe, then programmed Argus for a slight time delay. As Dr. Halstrom stood, she leaned on the cane.

She went down the hall to the Night Room, set the lights, and sat in the chair. For her, no straps were necessary. "So, Rolfe," she murmured as the lights dimmed. "So." She set the helmet on her head. After a few minutes, she heard the far-off sigh of wind through the trees.

THE NIGHT ROOM

A bird chirped as though in warning.

She should be at home, but instead she was outside on skis. The sun shone brilliantly on snow-covered slopes. "Ursula," a man's voice called. "Come on. Let's race back to the lodge!"

Understanding at last what was happening, she skied straight toward Rolfe. He was waving at her as she heard a sound like a faraway shot.

Faster, faster . . .

She reached him just as snow covered them both.

ABOUT THE AUTHOR

E. M. GOLDMAN became a writer so she could sit in a small room all day and stare at a computer screen. She is very pale. A Canadian, she is the author of *Money to Burn*, *Getting Lincoln's Goat*, and numerous science fiction and fantasy short stories.